The Fastest Boy in the World

Elizabeth Laird is the multi-award-winning author of several much-loved children's books. She has been shortlisted for the prestigious Carnegie Medal five times. She lives in Britain now, but still likes to travel as much as she can.

Also by Elizabeth Laird and published
by Macmillan Children's Books

The Fastest Boy in the World

Illustrated by
Peter Bailey

Elizabeth Laird

MACMILLAN CHILDREN'S BOOKS

First published 2014 by Macmillan Children's Books
a division of Macmillan Publishers Limited
20 New Wharf Road, London N1 9RR
Basingstoke and Oxford
Associated companies throughout the world
www.panmacmillan.com

ISBN 978-1-4472-6716-4 (HB)
ISBN 978-1-4472-6717-1 (PB)

Text copyright © Elizabeth Laird 2014
Illustrations copyright © Peter Bailey 2014

5 7 9 8 6 4

A CIP catalogue record for this book is available from
the British Library.

Printed and bound by CPI Group (UK) Ltd, Croydon CR0 4YY

For my grandson George

Chapter One

In my dreams I'm always running, running, running. Sometimes my feet fly over the ground and I'm sure that if I could just go a little bit faster I'd take off and fly like an eagle. Sometimes my legs feel as heavy as tree trunks, but I know that I must go on and reach the finishing line whatever it costs.

I've been running almost since I was a toddler. As soon as I could toddle, I'd stagger after my father as fast as my little legs would take me when he set out for the market on our donkey.

'Solomon! Come back!' my mother would shout. I wouldn't listen, so she'd have to run after me, snatch me up and laugh with me all the way home.

That was how my childhood began. And I can remember, as clearly as anything, the night when everything changed.

I was eleven years old. At least, I think I was eleven. In the countryside in Ethiopia, nobody takes much notice of how old you are.

It was the end of the day, and the door of our house was firmly shut. It always made me shiver to think of the night outside. Not just because it was dark and cold, but because there might be a hyena or two, lurking in the darkness, or, even worse, something – demonish.

I'll have to explain what our family home was like, in case you have never been to Ethiopia. It was round, like most other people's houses up there in our cool highlands, and it had a thatched roof that went up to a point. There was only one room, with the fire burning away in the middle. It got a bit smoky, but it kept us warm and gave a glowing light. There was a screen at one end, and our animals lived behind it – at night, that is. In the daytime, of course, they were out grazing.

Anyway, that evening Ma was stirring the pot of stew that was cooking over the fire. The smell was so good it was making me feel very hungry.

'How old am I, Ma?' I said suddenly. I don't know what put the idea into my head.

'Let me see,' she said vaguely, dropping another pinch of red-hot pepper into the pot. I could tell she wasn't listening.

Abba (that's what we called my father) *was*

listening, though. He had just come in from his work out on our farm. He sat down on a little stool beside the fire, and I could see he was as hungry as I was.

'You were born the year the harvest was so bad, and we had to borrow all that money from your uncle,' he said.

Ma looked reproachfully at him.

Abba blinked, and looked a bit guilty.

'I wasn't thinking,' he said quietly. 'It was Hailu who was born that year.'

Hailu was my older brother, but he died when he was little. Ma always sighs when anyone reminds her of him.

Abba shot her an understanding look, then he scratched his head.

'Oh no, I remember now,' he said. 'You were born the year the magician came and turned my stick into a wand of gold.'

I loved it when Abba was in his teasing mood. Konjit, my little sister, had been picking up the unburnt ends of twigs and throwing them on to the fire, while twisting a bit of hair over her forehead at the same time. She only ever seems to use one hand for anything useful. The other one is permanently fiddling with her hair. Now, though, she stopped for a whole long minute.

'Oh!' she said, her big brown eyes as round as the buttons on Grandfather's cotton jacket. 'A gold wand? Where is it?'

I nudged her, just to show that I knew she was being silly, then had to pull her upright in case she toppled over into the fire.

'It turned back into a stick again, just like that,' Abba said, giving me a sly look. 'Anyway, it wasn't that year. You were born just at the time when Twisty Horn had twins, only they didn't turn out to be calves but a couple of chickens. You should have seen them! They went flapping about all over the place.'

Everyone laughed, and even Grandfather, who had been sitting on the clay bench that ran right round the wall of the house, made a sort of rusty, wheezing sound that meant that he was laughing too, but Konjit didn't even smile. She looked quite shocked.

'Cows can't have chickens for babies, Abba,' she said seriously. 'Everyone knows that.'

She falls for it every time.

Just at that moment, a whiffling snort came from the stable behind the screen of sticks. I knew it was

Twisty Horn, and not Long Tail or Big Hoof. I know the sound of all our animals. I can tell our donkey (her name is Lucky) from all the other donkeys at the market just by the way she brays. I know our three dogs too, of course, but they don't come into the house with us. Their job is to stay outside and guard our farm. They pretty much look after themselves.

'You're quite right, darling. Cows only have calves,' said Abba, pulling Konjit sideways so that she could lean against his arm. I could tell his teasing mood was over. He was too tired for much when the evening came. He'd been out working all day on the farm.

'Supper's ready,' Ma said at last. She fetched out the big enamel tray and laid a huge round piece of pancake bread on it. (Our bread is called 'injera', and it's soft and thin and delicious.) Then she scooped spoonfuls of stew from the pot and set them out in front of each of our places.

Grandfather stood up and walked over to join us by the fire. I waited expectantly.

Five, I said to myself.

I counted the steps he was taking, and, sure enough, his knees cracked like breaking sticks at the fifth step.

(I like doing that – guessing numbers, I mean. It's a private game I play with myself, and with my friend Marcos, when he's in the right mood.)

Grandfather sat down on the little stool that Abba had pulled up for him.

'Solomon's eleven,' he said.

I'd forgotten by now that I'd asked about my age. It was my job to take the bowl and the little jug of water round so that everyone could wash their hands before they ate, yet I was too hungry to think about anything but food.

No one said much while we were eating, but when we'd had enough Grandfather sat back on his stool and said again, more thoughtfully this time, 'Solomon's eleven.'

I thought his mind was wandering, but it wasn't. He suddenly squared his shoulders, pulled the end of his thick white shawl away from his neck, as if he was too hot, and said, for the third time, 'Eleven. Quite old enough. We'll go tomorrow.'

My parents went quiet. Ma froze with her hand halfway up to her mouth. Abba had pulled his little tooth-cleaning stick from his inside pocket. He froze too.

'Go where?' whispered Konjit. She didn't dare

speak up in front of Grandfather. I knew she was burning to add, 'Wherever it is, can I come too?' but she would never have been so disrespectful. I was glad she'd asked the question, though, because I was burning to ask it too.

'To Addis Ababa,' said Grandfather, as casually as if he was talking about Kidame, our nearby town, where I go to school and Abba goes to the market on Thursdays. 'There's a man I need to see. Solomon can come with me. It's time he saw something of the world, and I might need him, anyway.'

My heart had started pumping, and my face felt as if it was on fire. Addis Ababa! Our capital city! Marcos's brother had been there once. He'd come home and told the most amazing stories, about huge buildings with walls of glass, and streets crowded with cars, and everyone wearing smart clothes, and staircases that moved. I'd never been further than Kidame. It's all right, I suppose, but it's only a small town. It's got one main street, which gets really muddy in the Big Rains. The bus comes through once a day, and cars sometimes too.

It was about five miles to my school. I usually ran all the way there in the mornings, because our teacher got furious if we were late. Then, of course,

I had to run all the way home again in the afternoon. Only sometimes I walked the last bit.

We weren't complete country bumpkins in Kidame. There was a shop in the main street so that if people needed anything they could buy it between Thursdays. Thursday was market day, and you could get practically anything in the market. There was electricity in Kidame too. There was even a TV in the bar. Marcos and I used to creep up to the window sometimes to watch it, and we usually got five or ten minutes in before the barman came and shooed us away.

Marcos even had electricity in his house. He could do his homework under a light in the evening, unlike me. Lucky him. I had to hold my books as near as I could to the fire. I could never see them very well, and they got all smudgy. If I held them too close, they even ended up singed. Marcos's house was near the pump too, where there was always running water. My mother had to fetch our water in a big heavy jar from the stream way down at the bottom of the hill every morning, with Konjit running after her, carrying her own little pot.

Anyway, to get back to the story.

Ma was still staring open-mouthed at Grandfather.

'How – how long will you . . . ?' she said to Grandfather, looking pleadingly at him.

'It's a day's walk,' Grandfather said. 'We'll start tomorrow at sun-up, and be there by sundown. You remember my nephew Wondu? We'll stay two nights with him near Piazza. Then we'll get the bus back to Kidame the following morning. Now no fuss, please. Solomon will be all right, and it's the school holidays at the moment so he won't miss any lessons.'

I loved the way he talked, in that casual, confident way about 'Piazza', wherever that was, and getting the bus home. A bus! I'd never been on a bus before.

Abba was looking worried.

'It's years and years since you were last in Addis Ababa, Father,' he said. 'How will you find your way? It's changed so much, I hear. And walking all that distance . . .'

'That's why I need Solomon,' Grandfather said briskly. 'I'm not done yet. It's only twenty-three miles. I've walked a lot further than that in one day in my time. But I'd rather have company, and Solomon will do just fine.'

I don't remember the rest of the evening. Ma fussed about whether my shirt was clean (I only have one, apart from my school uniform). Then she worried about what we were going to eat on the journey. Grandfather didn't take any notice. He was looking pleased with himself. He stood up, and went to lie down on the clay bench, folding his shawl over himself like a blanket. A minute later, he was asleep.

Abba nodded at me to come and sit beside him.

'I hadn't expected this, Solomon,' he said quietly, looking down into the still, glowing heart of the fire. 'I'd planned to take you to Addis Ababa myself one of these days. Now you be careful. Your grandfather is an old man and Addis Ababa is a very big city. He may not remember the way too well. Don't hurry or fuss him. Let him lean on you when he gets tired.'

He felt inside the pocket of his tunic, and brought out a little roll of tattered dollar bills. He peeled off a few of them, and put them into my hand.

'For emergencies,' he said. 'If your grandfather can't find his nephew, or if something goes wrong, you've got a little bit to help you out. Only if you really need it, mind. I know I can trust you not to lose it.'

I had never held so much money in my hands before. I felt quite frightened of it.

'There are thieves in Addis,' Abba went on,

looking serious. He nodded to Ma, who stood up and fetched down a little pouch from a shelf above the grain bins. Abba put the money in it and showed me how to hang it round my neck and keep it tucked inside my shirt.

'There, now mind you keep it safe,' Ma said. Her forehead was creased up with worry. I knew it was me she was anxious about, more than the money, and it made me feel a bit worried too.

The fire had died away to a few weak flames by

the time we lay down that night. I stared up into the dim shadows flickering around the rafters. I was too excited to sleep.

What would Marcos say when I told him I'd been to Addis? He'd be sick with envy. But then my stomach jumped.

What if I lost sight of Grandfather in the busy streets, among all the crowds of people? What if thieves attacked me and stole my money?

I'll be really, really careful, I told myself. *I'll look after Grandfather really well.*

Then, suddenly, I was asleep.

Chapter Two

The rooster woke me up with his crowing. He sat right on top of the house every morning, making his racket. I usually slept through it, and had to be shaken awake by Ma, but the rooster did his job that morning, and woke me out of my sleep.

Normally I knew it was time to get up because of the chinks of daylight showing between the sticks in the walls of our house, but this morning it was still dark, so I could tell that it was very early. Ma was up, though. She was leaning over the fire, blowing on the flames she had coaxed back to life, and the kettle was sitting on the hearthstones, singing away.

'Ma, did I dream it?' I said. 'Am I really going to Addis today?'

'Yes, you are,' she said grimly. 'And make sure you come back safe and sound.'

Grandfather had woken by now. He made a sort of groaning noise, like he always did when he sat up in the morning, then crossed himself and murmured a prayer.

'Come on, Workenesh,' he said to Mother. 'Where's my breakfast? We haven't got all day.'

Ma was ready for that. She poured a stream of golden liquid from the smoke-blackened kettle into a little glass and handed it to him. Grandfather sucked at it noisily. Ma gave me some too.

'Mind your manners in Addis Ababa, Solomon,' she said. 'Don't let those smart city people think you come from a bad home. Be respectful. Don't speak unless you're spoken to, and don't gobble your food.'

'That'll do, woman,' said Grandfather. 'Leave the boy alone.'

We were off soon afterwards. Abba and Ma stood at the door of the house with Konjit between them to watch us go.

It's one thing running by yourself along tracks you know so well that you could feel your way along them blindfold. It's quite another having to walk at the same speed as someone else, especially when that person is old.

I knew every inch of that run into Kidame. I had

my own counting games to help me make the miles go faster. I'd guess how many steps I'd need to get to the tree at the corner of the lane, and count the little brown birds sitting on the wall below the church (there were usually four or five) and I'd never forget to touch the big stone at the bottom of the hill to keep evil away. I'd do it all at lightning speed too.

Talking about running, I might as well explain that it was what I wanted to do more than anything else. Be a runner, I mean. Not just a boy who ran to school and back every day. I wanted to run in big races in other countries and bring glory to Ethiopia and make everyone in Kidame think I was a hero. I wanted to be the fastest runner in the world.

In Ethiopia, even the little kids in country places know about our famous Ethiopian runners. They're the best. World championships, marathons, the Olympic Games – they win medals wherever they go.

I knew you had to be super special to be a runner. You had to train, and train, and train, and run, and run, and run. You had to start really young.

But I did run and run. And, as I explained before, I'd started as soon as I could walk. I just didn't know how to train.

There's a school for runners in a town called Bekoji. It's only half a day on the bus from Kidame. Children go there to learn to run. I wanted desperately to go to that school.

I'd never dared tell Abba about wanting to be a runner. I knew he'd say no, because he needed me on the farm, but he couldn't stop me dreaming. No one can stop a person dreaming.

Anyway, there was no point in thinking about running while I was with Grandfather. He plodded along so slowly that I was burning with impatience. I was desperate to get past Kidame and on to see places I'd never been to before, along the road to Addis Ababa.

At first, I kept running ahead, then I'd have to stop and wait for Grandfather to catch up with me. He got irritated after a while.

'For goodness sake, Solomon,' he said. 'You're dancing about as if you've been stung by a bee. Calm down. Keep to the same pace, nice and steady, or you'll be exhausted before we get halfway.'

He was right, I suppose, but it took an age for us to get to Kidame, and even when we got there, Grandfather was in no hurry. He walked down the main street greeting all the other old men he met –

all his friends – and telling them he was off to Addis. At least it gave me the chance to do a bit of bragging myself, and by the time we were ready to walk out of town four or five boys from my school were there to wave me off, calling out silly things like, 'Bring me back a TV set! Make sure you get to watch a football match! Hop on a plane to America while you're about it, why don't you?'

Just as we were leaving town, Marcos came running after me.

'I've just heard, Solomon! They're flying back home today! They're landing in Addis tomorrow! You might see them! Oh, I wish, I wish I was coming with you!'

At least, I think that's what he was saying, only he was so excited and talking so fast that it sounded like, '. . . ear . . . fly . . . ome . . . Add . . . tomo . . . see . . . I wish!'

I stared at him and said, 'I don't know what you're talking about, you big idiot,' so he said it all again, and I got it this time.

'You mean the athletes? The runners? From the Olympics?'

'Yes!'

My heart gave a great kick. Our national heroes

Haile Gebrselassie! Derartu Tulu! I might really see them! In person!

I'd always imagined that the land beyond the hills on the far side of Kidame would be different and exciting, but it wasn't like that at all. Everywhere looked just like home, in fact, with little farmhouses dotted about among the fields, and a few trees, and the occasional round church with a tin roof and a cross on the top.

By the time the sun was overhead, we must have walked for about ten miles, and it was really hot. My legs were beginning to ache.

Grandfather was right about going slow and steady, I told myself.

Just when I thought I'd never be able to make it all the way, Grandfather said, 'We'll take a break in the next town and have something to eat.'

I won't go on about the rest of the journey. Just to say that it seemed to last forever. Twenty-three miles is no short stroll, after all. After a long time, the dirt road ended and we were walking along on smooth black stuff that Grandfather called 'tarmac'. There was more traffic now. Trucks came thundering up

behind us, blaring their horns, and once or twice a lumbering old bus roared past, puffing out choking black smoke from its rear end.

Every time we passed some houses, I'd say, 'Is this it, Grandfather? Is this Addis Ababa?'

And he'd say, 'This little village? Of course it isn't, you silly boy. Addis is much bigger than this.'

I didn't need to ask him when we got there at last. We were suddenly walking between big buildings, with glass windows that shone like fire in the setting sun. There were people everywhere, hurrying along the rough, stony ground at the side of the tarmac. There were rows of shops with signs outside them, some with meat hanging from hooks in the windows, some with piles of fruit in stands outside.

In Kidame, everyone knows everyone else, more or less, but in Addis people didn't stop to greet each other. They just rushed past.

I'd been so busy staring around at everything that I'd hardly noticed that we'd slowed right down. Grandfather had put his hand on my shoulder a while ago, and now I began to realize that he was leaning on me quite heavily.

I looked up into his face, and saw with a shock that it had gone a sort of grey colour. His lips were clamped tightly shut.

'Are you all right, Grandfather?' I asked him.

He grunted.

'Of course I am. Don't be cheeky.'

I wasn't being cheeky, and we both knew it. I was dog-tired myself, but now I was getting worried about Grandfather. What would I do if he stopped walking and couldn't go on?

I didn't have time to think too much because a big truck was careering down the road towards us. The roar of its engine was so loud that it blocked the sound of all the other traffic, so I didn't hear the other truck coming up behind us until it let out a deafening blast on its horn. I turned to look and saw that it was racing along half off the road, and coming straight for us, trying to give room for the oncoming truck to pass. Grandfather was right in its path. 'Grandfather, look out!' I shouted.

He didn't seem to hear me. I grabbed his arm and pulled him sideways. He fell to the ground with a crash. The truck roared past with another rude blast of its horn. Its wheels were only centimetres away from Grandfather's legs.

I squatted down beside him. I was afraid that he would be furious with me for pulling him over, but he didn't seem to notice that I was there. He was half sitting, half lying, and looked dazed.

'Are you hurt, Grandfather? Did it hit you? The truck?'

He stared back at me, but he didn't say anything.

'Grandfather!' My voice was rising. I was starting to feel panicky. Then he shook himself and said, in his usual grumbling voice, 'Not hit. No need to knock me down, though.'

I grinned, relieved. It was great to hear him speak, even though he was cross with me.

'Can you get up?' I put my hand under his elbow.

'Yes, yes. I don't need you,' he said irritably.

A little crowd of people had gathered. A man bent down and helped Grandfather to his feet.

'That truck driver,' he said. 'Outrageous. They think they own the place. Could have been a nasty accident.'

Grandfather tried to speak, but he seemed to be having trouble staying upright. A woman came up and took his arm.

'Come on over here, Uncle,' she said. 'You can sit down for a minute. Get your breath back.'

She took his arm and led him away from the road towards a little shop. A white plastic chair was set outside it against the wall. A young man was sitting on it, sliding a string of beads backwards and forwards between his fingers. The woman scowled at him and he stood up. Grandfather sank into the chair.

'Have you come far?' the woman asked me. 'The old man looks done in.'

'From Kidame.' I spoke as quietly as I could, to be polite, but I must have been too quiet.

'Never heard of it,' she said. 'Where are you going now?'

'My grandfather has a friend in a place called

Piazza,' I said, a bit louder. I felt shy. I wasn't used to being with strangers. The people around me were talking fast in a strange accent, rattling along in a way I could hardly understand. I stood like a block, afraid that I was looking stupid and ignorant.

'Piazza?' The man who had given Grandfather his chair laughed. 'That's right in the middle of town. You'd better get walking again, son, if you want to be there before midnight.'

The woman clucked at him.

'Don't be so hard-hearted, Yusuf. Can't you see the poor old man's exhausted? Walking all day, then practically run over, with only a child to help him. They should take the minibus. One'll be along in a minute.'

A bus! The thought of it scared me. How could I ever find the right bus? How much would a ride on it cost? Was this the kind of emergency Abba had meant? And how would we know where to get off?

The woman seemed to read my thoughts.

'First time in the city, are you? I know what that's like. I come from the country myself. Don't worry, dear. The bus only costs a few cents. And everyone gets off at Piazza. You can't go wrong. Yusuf will take you to the bus stop and help you get on it.'

She turned on the man with a ferocious scowl.

'Stop looking so grumpy, you big lump,' she barked at him. 'You've been sitting on that chair doing nothing all afternoon. Make yourself useful for once.'

My mouth fell open. I'd never heard a woman talk to a man like that before. Was that what people did in Addis Ababa?

'I nearly said, *Thank you very much, ma'am, but we'll walk. I'm sure my grandfather will be all right in a minute*, but when I looked at Grandfather I could see that he wasn't all right at all.

'What shall we do, Grandfather?' I whispered to him. 'She says we ought to go on a bus.'

He licked his dry lips and nodded.

'Bus,' he croaked.

The woman had disappeared inside. She came out again with a glass of water.

'Here, drink this, Uncle,' she said. 'It'll make you feel better.'

And she was right, because when Grandfather had gulped the water down he looked more like his old self. He got to his feet, leaned on his stick (gripping the top of it so hard that his knuckles went pale), made a little bow then began a speech of thanks.

She cut him short.

'Yes, well, it's nothing. We're all God's children. Get on now, with Yusuf. He'll show you where the bus stops and put you on it. You take care of your grandfather, young man. No more long walks for a day or two, eh?'

Chapter Three

The bus to Piazza was much smaller than the big red ones that rumble in and out of Kidame. It was packed tight with people already.

'It's full,' I said, hanging back, but Yusuf gave me a shove in the back, and I shot in through the door almost into the lap of a fat lady with a black scarf tied round her head.

My face went hot with embarrassment, but I didn't have time to think about it, because then Yusuf gave Grandfather a push, and he almost landed on top of her too.

Somehow or other, everyone shuffled up a bit, and Grandfather got to sit down properly, with me squashed between him and the fat lady. Then the boy by the door slid it shut with a slam and we were off.

It was awful. I couldn't help leaning on the fat lady, and she kept prodding me with her elbows muttering with annoyance, and the bus set off with a roar, then lurched about all over the place. Nobody seemed to think there was anything odd about it. I couldn't imagine how people lived like this all the time. I was worried about paying the fare because I had no idea how much money it would cost. I started trying to pull the money pouch out from inside my shirt. Luckily, Grandfather knew what to do. He fished some coins out of his pocket and gave them to the boy, who accepted them with a nod.

It was stuffy in the bus. I didn't mind the smell of hot people, but the petrol fumes were disgusting and I thought I was going to be sick.

I can't be sick, I told myself. *I mustn't be sick. Please don't let me be sick!*

Just when I thought I'd have to be, the boy by the door called out 'Piazza!' and the bus jerked to a stop, and the door slid open and everyone tumbled out.

I'd been dreading this bit. I kept remembering what Abba had said, about Grandfather being old, and how he hadn't been in Addis Ababa for years, and how I would have to look after him.

I can't look after him! I thought, feeling panicky. *I can't look after myself! I don't know where we are, or where to go!*

I needn't have worried after all. Grandfather had

settled his shawl back round his shoulders and now he looked ready to set off.

'Don't stand there gawping, Solomon,' he said. 'Come here. What do you expect me to lean on. Thin air?'

Then he set off, his hand clamped on to my shoulder, and we pushed our way through the crowds of people.

I felt worse than I'd felt all day. My feet hurt, my ears buzzed with the noise of the people and the traffic, and my stomach was still churning after the ride in the bus.

Are we nearly there, Grandfather? I wanted to ask, but I didn't because it would have sounded childish.

But then Grandfather's hand twisted on my shoulder as he pushed me out of the big crowded street and down a little lane. He stopped.

'Is this it?' I said.

He didn't answer, and looking up I saw something I'd never seen before. Grandfather was unsure of himself. He looked smaller all of a sudden, and older.

We'd stopped outside a corrugated iron fence, and as we stood there a door in it opened and a man stepped out. He looked about the same age as my father.

Grandfather cleared his throat.

'Good day,' he said, in a voice that sounded almost quavery. 'Is this the house of Mr Wondu?'

The man was setting off up the lane, but he stopped and turned.

'Yes.'

It was evening already and the light had almost gone. The man leaned forward to look closely at Grandfather.

'Uncle Demissie! Is that you?'

I felt almost weak with relief and I could tell that Grandfather did too.

'Wondu, my boy, it's you, isn't it?'

They clasped each other's hands, and touched shoulders, right, then left, then right. But, even in the dim light, I could see what Grandfather couldn't – my father's cousin looked as if he'd had a nasty shock.

He looks almost scared of us, I thought. *He wishes we hadn't come, anyway.*

Cousin Wondu seemed to pull himself together and managed a weak smile.

'Come in, Uncle,' he said, leading us into his compound. 'Where have you come from? Have you travelled far today?'

'Only from home,' Grandfather said.

We had crossed the little patch of bare earth in front of the house, and now Cousin Wondu was opening the door.

'And how was the journey? I suppose the bus was jam-packed. Did it break down? It always does when I travel out of Addis.'

He's laughing at us, I thought. *He thinks we're ignorant.*

'What bus? We walked, of course,' Grandfather said. His sharpness usually scared me, but I was glad to hear it in his voice now.

'You . . . walked?'

Wondu sounded astonished.

A woman had pushed aside the bead curtain that covered a door at the back of the room. She had a narrow face and a sharp look in her eyes. She started in alarm when she saw us, and pushed away the little girl who was holding on to her skirt.

'Meseret, you remember Uncle Demissie?' said Cousin Wondu. 'It's wonderful to see him after all this time, isn't it?'

He sounded almost pleading.

'You're welcome,' said Cousin Meseret unwillingly. 'Who's this?'

All eyes turned on me. I stood there, feeling stupid, a hot flush spreading right through me.

'He's Solomon. My grandson,' Grandfather said shortly.

'He walked all the way from Kidame too?' Cousin Wondu didn't seem able to believe it.

'Of course he did,' said Grandfather. 'It's nothing to a boy his age. When I was eleven, I . . .'

And he started on one of his rambling stories. All I could think was, *When are they going to give us a drink and something to eat?*

They did at last, of course. There was a lot of bustling about, and I heard sharp words from Cousin Meseret who was in the kitchen behind the living room. She was telling Cousin Wondu what to do. I was a bit shocked, quite honestly. Ma would never have talked to Abba like that. At last Cousin Wondu came out with some bottles of orange soda for us to drink. (I was glad I'd had a fizzy drink once at Marcos's house, or the bubbles would have given me a real surprise.) He looked nervous as he fumbled with the bottle opener.

'You'll stay here with us, of course,' Cousin Wondu said, shooting a glance at his wife, who nodded, smiling stiffly.

Something inside me relaxed. I hadn't realized how worried I'd been about where we were going to sleep that night.

Yes! I thought triumphantly. *We've made it! We're here!*

I don't remember much more about that evening because as soon as we'd had supper (and it was a nice one too, with plenty of meat), I felt so sleepy that I could hardly keep my eyes open. I did hear Grandfather say, 'It's only for a couple of nights, Wondu. There's a man I have to see tomorrow. We'll be going home the day after that.'

And I saw the relief in Cousin Wondu's eyes as he said unconvincingly, 'Stay as long as you like, Uncle. You know that my house is your house.'

Chapter Four

Nothing would have kept me awake that night. I think I was asleep before I even lay down on the mat that Cousin Wondu had laid out for me on the floor.

The rooms in Cousin Wondu's house were full of furniture. You had to be careful all the time not to bump into things. We don't have furniture at home, except for a couple of stools.

A squeaking noise and a metal clang woke me up at last. I felt a shock of fright when I opened my eyes. The light was so bright! It poured into this strange room through glass windows.

I sat up. Grandfather's bed was empty. The clanging noise must have come from when he'd opened the metal door to go out. I groaned as I stood up. Every bit of me was stiff, and my feet felt sore.

Cousin Wondu and Grandfather were sitting at the table, and Grandfather was drinking a glass of tea. The little girl I'd seen the night before was staring at him with her mouth hanging open. She was wearing a pink dress made of frills that stuck out all around her. I wished Konjit could have seen it. Her eyes would have popped right out of her head.

Grandfather cleared his throat and the little girl jumped back with fright.

'Say good morning to Uncle,' Cousin Wondu said in a jolly voice, pushing her forward.

She wasn't having any of that. She scuttled off into the room with the big bed in it and slammed the door behind her.

'She keeps us all in order,' said Cousin Wondu, with a soft smile.

I looked at Grandfather. I knew he wouldn't approve of that. It was never too early, in his view, to train children to be respectful. I thought he'd be frowning, but I could see that he'd hardly noticed the little girl. He just looked ill. There was a grey tinge to his skin, and his eyes seemed to have sunk deeper into his head.

Cousin Wondu had noticed too.

'You should rest, Uncle,' he said. 'Have a quiet day. Leave your business till tomorrow.'

Grandfather shook his head, as I knew he would.

'No need to fuss,' he growled. 'Nothing wrong with me.' He felt under his shawl and pulled out a crumpled paper, folded small. 'Look at this, Wondu. "Happiness Pastry". How do I find it?'

Cousin Wondu gave a sort of twitch. He bit his lip and shot a sideways look at Cousin Meseret. She just shrugged and stared back at him blankly.

'You want to eat some pastries, Uncle?' he said at last, turning back to us. 'But there's no need to run around town. Meseret can go out and buy some for you.' He pushed the plate of rolls towards Grandfather. 'Please, have some breakfast. You too, Solomon. Look, there's honey. It's very good. The best.'

His voice was soothing, as if he was talking to a child. I hated that. But Grandfather just waved his hand. He could have been swatting a fly.

'If you don't know where it is, Wondu,' he said, 'I'll find someone who does.'

I couldn't understand all this business about the Happiness Pastry. Anyway I was looking longingly at the plateful of rolls on the table. White bread! I'd hardly ever had that before. I felt too shy to help myself, but Grandfather gave me a curt nod.

'Eat up, Solomon. We've got to get going.'

Cousin Wondu had been biting his lip.

'Why don't you let me help you, Uncle?' he said

with a bright smile. 'I'll go out and find the pastry shop for you! It might be miles away at the other end of Addis. You'll exhaust yourself, wandering about all day. I'll go and find it, and tell you where it is, or, better still, take a message for you, if there's someone there you want to see.'

Something was up with Cousin Wondu. He was trying too hard, I could tell. I knew the look on his face. Marcos looked like that when he was telling his dad that we were going to do our homework together under the tree in the school compound, when really we were just going to kick an old ball around.

He doesn't care about Grandfather getting tired, I thought. *He doesn't want us to find this pastry place. But why not?*

I wanted to give Grandfather a warning nudge, but I didn't have to. He wasn't a sharp city person, like Cousin Wondu, but he wasn't an easy one to fool, either, as I knew all too well.

'Very good of you, my boy,' he said, nodding as if he was pleased, 'but you'll be wanting to get off to work I expect. We'll look forward to seeing you later. Come along, Solomon, or are you planning to sit there stuffing your face all day?'

Cousin Wondu looked desperately at Cousin Meseret, and she said, 'But it'll be awful out in town today. The Olympic athletes are landing at the airport this morning and the streets will be packed. There's going to be a procession of triumph through the whole city. You'll never be able to get anywhere.'

Cousin Wondu leaped on this.

'She's right. Honestly, Uncle, we'll be worried about you if you go out today.'

I could have told him to save his breath. Nothing stops Grandfather doing what he wants to do, and for once I was glad of it. A procession of triumph! I might get to see it. To see *them*! And, if I did, everyone in Kidame would just about die of envy.

We were out in the street soon after that. Cousin Wondu was still protesting, even as we went out through the door, but Grandfather just ignored him. My feet were still sore from the day before, and my legs ached too, but I forgot about them as soon as we came out of Cousin Wondu's side street on to the main road.

I was busy looking around at everything, at the cars, and the buildings, and the people. I was confused by all the noises too, the blaring horns,

and rumbling trucks, and shouting people. Cousin
Wondu had been right. The streets were much more
crowded than they'd been the day before. Everyone
was waiting for the procession to come past.

Suddenly I realized that I'd lost Grandfather. For
a moment I was too frozen with fright to move, and
then the gang of schoolgirls in front of me parted,
and I caught sight of his grey head walking along in
his calm, unhurried way. I ran to catch up with him
and felt a babyish urge to hold on to his hand, but of
course I didn't.

'Where are we going, Grandfather?' I asked.
'How are we going to find this place?'

He didn't like questions, so I might have saved
myself the bother of asking, because I knew all the
time that he wouldn't answer. Instead, he headed
over towards a little shop, not one of the smart ones
with big glass windows, but a little one that looked
as if it had wandered into the city from the country,
like us.

An old man was sitting on a bench outside it,
enjoying the warmth of the morning sun. Grandfather
went up to him and coughed politely to attract his
attention. The old man looked up.

It took a long time, of course. It always does

when old men get together. All the greetings, and introductions and explanations – they never seem to stop. When Grandfather sat down on the bench beside the old man, and they got started on the state of the roads in Addis Ababa, I thought we'd be there all day.

Grandfather got to the point at last.

'The Happiness Pastry?' the old man said, holding Grandfather's crumpled bit of paper close up to his eyes. 'Yes, I know where that is. Not far from here at all. I'll get my nephew to show you the way.'

He twisted round to call back in through the open door of the shop.

'Kebede! Where is that dratted boy? Come here!'

A boy came out. He looked about my age.

'Show this gentleman the way to the Happiness Pastry,' the old man ordered, 'then come straight back here.'

'Yes, Uncle,' the boy said, but when he saw me looking at him, he gave me a sly grin. I almost laughed out loud. He'd be off on a nice little expedition of his own once he'd shown us the way – I was sure of it.

I thought I'd feel shy with a smart city boy like Kebede, who was wearing shoes and new-looking

shorts, but he was so friendly that I liked him at once.

'Is this the way they'll come? The athletes?' I asked him.

'Sure,' he said. 'What do you think everyone's waiting for?'

I still couldn't believe that I was actually going to see them. Derartu Tulu and Haile Gebrselassie had been my heroes ever since I could remember. They seemed supernatural to me, not like real people at all. I'd never imagined, in my wildest dreams, that I might actually ever see them in real life.

'Here you are,' Kebede said suddenly. 'The Happiness Pastry.'

His uncle had been right. It had taken hardly any time at all to find it.

'Good lad,' Grandfather said. He fished out a coin from his pocket and gave it to Kebede. 'Get back to your shop now.'

With a polite thank you and a wink at me, Kebede had gone.

I looked above the doorway of the pastry shop. A large sign said 'Happiness'. It could be seen from away down the street, in both directions.

Cousin Wondu must know this place, I said to myself. *I wonder what he's up to?*

Chapter Five

I'd been excited at the thought of the pastry shop. There's no such thing in Kidame, but I knew about sweet cakes because Marcos's uncle had brought some when he'd come to visit his family. Marcos said he'd never eaten anything like those cakes in his whole life. He said they stuck to his teeth, but in a nice way. I wasn't silly enough to expect Grandfather to buy me one, of course, but I suppose there was a lurking hope at the back of my mind.

As it was, I didn't even have time to take a proper look in through the door. All I got was a glimpse of a shiny floor, some metal chairs and tables and a glass counter with piles of yellow, brown and white cakes on shelves underneath.

It wasn't the Happiness Pastry shop that Grandfather wanted to visit after all, but the building beside it. This was high, with shops on the ground floor and four storeys above. Grandfather pushed open a door at the side and began to walk slowly up the staircase. When the door clanged shut behind us, I'll admit right now that my nerves were tingling. I'd never been in a place like this before. As a matter of fact, I wasn't exactly used to stairs. In Kidame even our school is all on one floor.

I followed Grandfather up step by step, going as slowly as he did. On every landing there were doors off to the left and the right, and Grandfather stopped, gasping for breath, pointing to the plaques on them to make me read them out to him. They were all in English, and he's better at reading Amharic.

'Blue Nile Insurance,' I spelled out. 'Ghion Export. Lion Trading.'

Every time, Grandfather shook his head, sighed, and plodded on upward.

At last we came to a door that just said 'Ethiopian Sports Company', and when I'd read it out to him Grandfather gave a grunt of triumph that turned into a cough. I can tell you, if you're interested, that we'd climbed sixty-nine steps.

I looked round and saw that he was holding on to the banister and his face had that grey look on it again. There was nothing I could do, so I just waited until he had stopped panting.

'Is this it, Grandfather? Are you all right?'

He didn't answer, but he reached out for my shoulder and, leaning on me, walked the few steps to the door. It opened just before we reached it and a smart young woman in a red dress came rushing out, a handbag swinging from her shoulder. She clattered off down the stairs in her high-heeled shoes. Even though she'd barely glanced at me, she'd made me feel like a worm. I was horribly conscious of my bare feet and crumpled shirt and stained old shorts.

I think that, just for once, Grandfather must have guessed how I was feeling, because he squeezed my elbow and said, 'City girls, eh, Solomon? They all think they're the Queen of Sheba.'

Then he squared his shoulders and marched me into the office.

It took a while for him to explain himself, and we had to put up with quite a few stares and raised eyebrows from the five people sitting behind desks, who were reading piles of paper, or clattering away on keyboards, or staring into screens, or talking on telephones. It was then that I heard Ato Alemu's name for the first time. At last, though, they waved us towards a bench at the side of the room.

I still hadn't got any idea of what Grandfather

wanted, or why we'd come to this place, and as we sat and waited, on and on, I started to wonder if Grandfather had any idea either. Old people did get mixed up about things sometimes, I knew. Perhaps we'd come all this way to Addis for some crazy reason after all.

I should have had more faith in my wily old grandfather because at last a door at the end of the room opened and a man came out. He looked at us without smiling. He seemed a bit cautious, as if he was afraid we'd turn out to be a nuisance. He was about the same age as Abba and Cousin Wondu, I know that now, but he looked much younger and he couldn't have been more different. He was wearing a brilliant white shirt and a blue tie and his shoes were shiny with polish. His hands were smooth, not a bit like Abba's powerful, rough, working hands, and he had a big gold ring on one finger. I could see a silver-coloured watch too, poking out from beneath his shirt sleeve.

'So you're Ato Demissie, are you?' he said, frowning. He looked down at me. 'Did this boy bring you here? You can go now, son,' and he started feeling in his pocket for a coin.

Grandfather was still struggling to get up from

the bench and the effort was making him mutter irritably.

'This is my grandson, Solomon,' he wheezed out. 'Are you really Alemu, Petros's son?'

The man's frown deepened. He nodded curtly.

'You'd better come into my office.'

He led us across the room, with the eyes of all the people behind their desks following us curiously, and in through the door of his office, which he closed behind us.

Chapter Six

There were three armchairs at one end of the room, set round a small table. I sat down nervously on the edge of my chair. I was afraid of leaving marks on it. Ato Alemu reached over to his desk and pressed a button on it. At once, one of the smart girls from the office outside came in.

'Soft drinks, coffee,' Ato Alemu said, without looking at her. He was staring at Grandfather. I thought it was a bit rude of him, and was afraid that Grandfather would lose his temper.

'So you're the Arrow,' he said.

Grandfather sat back in his chair and his face broke open into the brightest smile I'd ever seen on it.

'That's what the boys used to call me. And they called your father the Bullet.'

Ato Alemu's face changed at once. The doubtful look vanished right out of his eyes, and he looked really excited. I thought he was going to jump out of his chair.

'You really *are* the Arrow! You must be! Only you would have known my father's nickname. I thought you were . . . Oh, I'm so happy to see you, Ato Demissie. It's an honour to meet you at last. You and my father! Fastest runners in His Majesty's Bodyguard! In the whole Ethiopian army! You're very welcome, sir. More than I can say.'

My eyes were swivelling from one to the other. Arrow? Bullet? What on earth was going on?

Ato Alemu seemed to read my thoughts.

'Didn't you know that your old granddad had been a famous runner once upon a time?' he said, and he reached forward to slap me on the shoulder.

I shook my head shyly.

'And a soldier in the Emperor's elite Bodyguard?'

Well, I'd heard of the Emperor, of course. Haile Selassie. Everyone still calls him 'His Majesty'. He'd been the ruler of Ethiopia for years and years, until the revolution had thrown him out. That was before even Abba was born. The revolutionaries had killed Haile Selassie, then they'd rounded up thousands and thousands of other people and murdered them too. It had been a horrible time in Ethiopia. No one likes to talk about it, except to be glad that the reign of terror is over.

'Yes,' Ato Alemu was still saying. The Bullet and
the Arrow. My dad and your grandfather. The fastest
two men in the army.'

He turned back to Grandfather.

'It's wonderful that you've come to see me, Ato
Demissie! But how did you find me?'

Grandfather shook his head sadly.

'It was because I heard about your father's death.
I was sorry.'

The smile fell from Ato Alemu's face.

'It was very sudden. Just a week of illness. We did
everything we could. Doctors, medicines . . .'

'I don't doubt it.' Grandfather looked sadder than
I'd ever seen him. 'The Bullet, eh? The Bullet . . .'

His voice tailed away.

'But how . . . ?' Ato Alemu prompted him gently.

Grandfather cleared his throat.

'Your father wrote to me last year, before the Big
Rains. He didn't know where to find me of course,
but he sent me a letter through friends. He thought
it was safe enough to look for me, I suppose, now
that all this time has passed. The letter went from
one person to another, and then someone in Kidame
handed it to me, three weeks ago. That person told
me that I was too late to meet up with your father

again, and that he'd died. He told me where to find
you too.'

The girl came in with a tray of drinks. She smiled
at me as she put the tray down on the table.

You've changed your tune, I thought, feeling
triumphant. She'd scowled at us as if we'd been a
couple of old beggars when we'd been out there
in the office. It was different now that we were
obviously the boss's honoured guests.

Grandfather took a glass of tea from the tray and
I daringly helped myself to a bottle of orange soda.
Ato Alemu leaned forward, his eyes shining with
interest.

'How long were you in prison, the two of you?
My father would never talk about it.'

Grandfather in prison? My mind reeled at the
idea.

'Five years,' Grandfather said. 'Nearly six. Brutal,
it was. Starving us, beatings . . .'

'Father never said much. Only that you'd saved
his life.'

Grandfather drained his glass.

'Anyone would have done the same.'

'That's not what Father told me. You attacked
the guard who was killing him, he said. You laid

him out cold. They'd have executed you for that, if they'd caught you.'

A slow smile spread over Grandfather's face.

'Yes, but they didn't catch me, did they?'

Ato Alemu sat back and clapped his hands in the air with delight.

'You really did that thing, didn't you? What my father said. You jumped off the back of a moving truck on to a galloping horse, and escaped.'

My mouth had fallen wide open. I'd never heard anything like this. I could never have *imagined* anything like this.

'Well,' Grandfather was saying with a cackle of laughter, 'the horse wasn't exactly galloping. More of a trot. And the truck was going quite slowly.'

'Tell me everything, Ato Demissie, please,' begged Ato Alemu. 'I've always wanted to know the whole story.'

Grandfather settled his shawl round his shoulders and cleared his throat. I was hugging myself inside with a sort of joyful pride.

'It was simple, really,' Grandfather began. 'Your father and I were arrested as soon as the revolution got underway. We'd been in His Majesty's Bodyguard, after all, so they knew we'd be loyal to our Emperor.

They put us in prison in Addis at first. It was hard, but . . .' He shrugged. 'We both survived. Many didn't. But Bullet, your father, he was unlucky. He made an enemy of one of the guards. Not for any reason. The man just picked him out. He was brutal. Merciless. The worst kind of bully. Your father didn't tell you about all that, and I won't, either.

'In the end, they decided to move us out of Addis to a labour camp way out in the country. They used to load us up in trucks every morning and drive us out to a quarry, where we had to break stones with useless hammers. In the evenings, when we were half dead with exhaustion and hunger, they'd drive us back to the camp again.

'We were on our way back at the end of a long miserable day, when something happened. I don't know what it was. Bullet must have said something, or laughed – I don't know. Anyway, this guard went crazy. He launched himself on Bullet and attacked him savagely. I thought he was going to strangle him. There was a hammer on the floor of the truck beside me, and I just picked it up and hit him on the head. The guard fell like a stone. I knew I'd killed him. I knew I had to get away at once.'

'You didn't kill him,' Ato Alemu said. 'You

cracked his skull, but he lived. He never quite recovered, though. At least, he was never going to bully anyone again.'

It was Grandfather's turn to stare at Ato Alemu. At last he cleared his throat and said, 'Thank you, son. You've relieved my mind of a terrible fear. All these years, I thought I was a murderer.'

I was dying to ask Grandfather what had happened next, but I didn't dare say a word. Luckily, Ato Alemu asked for me.

'Well,' said Grandfather, 'luckily, I was at the back of the truck, next to the open end, and before the other guards could get at me I'd got one leg over the tailboard. And this horse – it was God who sent it to save my life – must have been spooked by the roar of the truck's engine, and it had broken away from the farmer who was leading it on a rein. It was right underneath the tailboard. So I jumped down on to it (I nearly fell off it, mind you), and I must have scared that poor horse so much that it bolted like lightning. It raced back down the road, then veered off into the countryside. As soon as we'd got a good long way away, I slid off it and began to run. I ran and ran. I heard shouts and shots in the distance behind me, but they never caught up with me. I set

off to walk by a long way round back to our family farm. It took weeks and weeks, hiding out all the way. I arrived almost starved, but my family looked after me. They kept me hidden for a while, until the immediate danger had passed. I just stayed quietly at home, not telling anyone anything, keeping an eye out, until the nightmare in our country was over, and we could all walk with our heads held high again. And that's the whole story, Alemu. That's how it happened.'

Chapter Seven

I didn't listen to the next bit of the conversation. Grandfather was asking about what had happened to the Bullet during all those years, and how he'd died and everything. I needed the time to get my head round what I'd just heard.

All my life, Grandfather had been there, living with us in our house, helping round the farm a bit, but spending most of his time sitting on a stump of wood outside the door, looking out across the countryside. He would walk into Kidame once a week or so, and stay for a few hours talking to the other old men. He'd pick up bits of news that way. But nobody ever came to visit him.

Kidame is a small place and everyone knows everyone else's business. Grandfather must have kept quiet about his old adventures, because if even one person had known it would have been all over town, and I'd have heard about it too.

I was trying to imagine what Grandfather might

have been like when he was young. Did he look like me? He must have been an amazing sight in his Bodyguard uniform. He must have been incredibly strong, and brave, too, to survive the labour camp, and then jump out of the truck straight on to that horse, and find his way home.

I wasn't surprised by how he went for that guard, because I knew he had a temper. He loses it at home over little things all the time. He's beaten me too, often, when he thought I was being cheeky.

The thing that had surprised me most was that he'd had a friend. A best friend. A man he was ready to die for. I'd never have thought that Grandfather would have had feelings like that.

'What was that? What did you say?' My head jerked up. I'd stopped listening, but Grandfather sounded so sharp that he'd brought me back to the present. 'My nephew Wondu came here? With that wife of his? To see you?'

'Yes.' Ato Alemu was nodding. 'I thought it was a little strange. There was something about him . . . As a matter of fact, he told me that you had died last year.'

Grandfather snorted.

'That boy! He's a tricky one. I've always known

it. Too much like his devious father. I could never trust him and he was my own brother. Well, he's dead now, and I hope that God will rest his soul. But I, as you can see, am very much alive. What did Wondu mean by saying I was dead? What did he want from you?'

'Well,' said Ato Alemu slowly, 'I suppose it was my fault for saying too much. I've known Wondu slightly for years. We were students at the Business School at the same time. And then a few weeks ago, at some party or other, he happened to tell me that his family had come from around Kidame. My father had told me that you came from that part of the country, so I asked him if he knew you.

' "Old Demissie?" he said. "Yes, he's my uncle."

'I told him that I really wanted to find you, because you'd been my father's best friend, and before he died my father had given me something to give to you. Something valuable that had belonged to the Arrow, all those years ago. I told him that my father had kept it for you and wanted to return it to you.'

Grandfather nodded with satisfaction, as if he'd been hoping for something and his wish had been fulfilled.

'Later on, at the end of the party,' Ato Alemu

went on, 'I met Wondu and his wife by the door as they were leaving. She looked up at me with a pretty smile and said, "Wondu's told me something exciting. You've got a family treasure to give to his uncle."

'There was something too eager about her. She was trying to be charming, but she didn't fool me. She was a sharp one, I could tell. Runs rings round poor Wondu.

'"Sentimental value only," I told her, "but if Wondu can find out how to reach his uncle I'll send it on to him."

'Someone else was coming up behind us, trying to get through the door, so we all split up and went out into the street.'

This was all getting too deep for me. I was struggling to hang on to the thread. What was this mysterious thing that Ato Alemu was talking about? Was it a kind of treasure? Money? A hoard of gold? My ideas were getting bigger and bigger. Were we going to be rich?

'I've often wondered if he'd done it.' Grandfather was smiling broadly. 'He'd promised that he'd try, if anything happened to me. But how did he manage to dig it up out of the place where I'd buried it, smuggle it out of the prison camp and hang on to it all those years? He must have known how dangerous it would have been if they'd found it on him.'

'He did,' Alemu said, 'but he said he owed it to you. He knew how precious it was. And you'd saved his life.'

'Oh please! What is it? What are you talking about?'

I was unable to keep quiet any longer but I might as well have saved my breath, because they both ignored me anyway. Grandfather's face had gone dark with anger.

'So Wondu and Meseret came to see you,' he said. 'I think I know why. They wanted to get my father's heirloom off you. I suppose my brother had told him about it. He was always resentful that our father had given it to me.'

'It was only last week when they came,' Ato Alemu said. 'Wondu told me that his Uncle Demissie had passed away, and if I would give him whatever it was he'd make sure it went to your son, his cousin. I thought at the time that there was something a little odd about him. He didn't seem happy at all. That wife of his, Mrs Meseret, kept butting in and finishing his sentences for him.'

'But you didn't give him anything, did you?' I broke in. 'You didn't trust him.'

This time, they both turned to look at me. I think they'd forgotten I was there.

'You're a sharp one, Solomon,' Ato Alemu said with a laugh. 'No, I didn't give it to him. I decided that as soon as I had some free time I'd make the journey down to Kidame and visit the Arrow's family myself.'

Grandfather seemed to have forgotten about Cousin Wondu. He was shaking his head wonderingly.

'So the Bullet kept it for me, after all. He hinted at it in his letter without saying exactly what it was he had to give me. I suppose he realized that he didn't have long to go, and wanted to get it to me before he died. What a man. There'll never be another one like him.'

Ato Alemu stood up and walked round behind his desk.

'I've got it here,' he said. 'I'll give it to you now.'

Chapter Eight

The moment had come at last. Ato Alemu opened a drawer in his desk and took out a battered little box, not much bigger than a matchbox. He put it into Grandfather's hands.

I was so excited I could hardly breathe. I was dying for Grandfather to open it so that I could see what was inside, but he only gave it a little shake, and then held it still for an agonizing few minutes.

'Well,' he said. 'Well. After all this time.'

And then at last, when I thought I was going to burst with curiosity, he slid the lid of the box open. I leaned forward as far as I dared, craning my neck, my eyes on stalks.

What a let-down! There was no yellow gleam of gold, no sparkle of jewels, nothing except for a flat brown piece of metal with a head stamped on it.

What is it? What's so special about it? I was dying to say.

It was Ato Alemu who took pity on me.

'This, Solomon,' he said, 'is the Distinguished Military Medal of Haile Selassie the First. It was awarded by the Emperor to your grandfather's father for—'

'Acts of extreme gallantry,' broke in Grandfather. 'His Majesty pinned this medal to my father's chest with his own hands, just before I was born.'

Grandfather had a father? was all I could think. I knew of course that he must have had one. Everyone in the world has a father. But I'd never heard anything about him. It was a weirdly strange idea.

'My – my great-grandfather was a soldier too, then?' I asked.

As usual, Grandfather didn't answer me properly.

'Extreme gallantry,' he repeated. 'They were heroes then, all of them, fighting to send the Italian invaders out of our country. But my father was one of the best.'

'So this – what is it – medal – it's valuable, then? Like you said?'

I couldn't see how it could be, a little, brown, dull thing like that.

'Oh, it's valuable all right,' Ato Alemu answered. 'These things are very rare. There are collectors who'll pay a lot for them.'

'Is that why Cousin Wondu wanted it?' I persisted. 'To sell it?'

Grandfather shut the box with a snap.

'Wondu!' He sounded really disgusted. 'He's not getting his hands on this. It's not for sale. Not now, not ever. This stays in the family. *My* family. My father gave it to me when I entered His Majesty's Bodyguard. "Demissie," he said to me. "Take it to the barracks with you. Keep it safe. It'll bring you luck one day."'

Questions were boiling around in my head. I knew that Grandfather wouldn't have patience with all of them, so I chose the one I most wanted answered.

'But why did you have to hide it, Grandfather, when you were in the labour camp?'

He opened the lid of the box again, and thrust the medal in front of my face.

'See that head? You know who that is? It's His Majesty, Haile Selassie. What do you think those crazy revolutionaries would have done if they'd found an image of their great enemy on me? People were shot every day for much less than that.'

'So you kept it hidden, Grandfather. You showed the Bullet, though.'

'My comrade in arms,' Grandfather said stiffly. 'My comrade in everything.'

He stowed the medal away again, and set his hands down on the table, ready to heave himself to his feet.

'Very good of you, Alemu, to take such care of this for me. Bullet's son, eh? Chip off the old block.'

'Thank you, sir,' said Ato Alemu, looking pleased. 'He was a great man, my father.'

Outside, car horns suddenly started blaring. The procession of athletes must be coming! It must be nearly here! I held my breath. Was I going to miss it? Would Grandfather keep me stuck here in the office, while the greatest thing I would ever see in my whole life was happening down there in the street?

I should have trusted Grandfather. He was struggling to get to his feet, ready to leave. Ato Alemu put out a hand to stop him.

'Don't go yet, Uncle,' he said. The streets will be crowded. Wait till the procession has passed.'

He'd said 'Uncle' without seeming to notice. It was as if he'd become a member of our family. I could see that it had pleased Grandfather. But I knew a crowded street wouldn't stop him when he'd decided to go.

'No,' he said, managing to stand upright at last. 'We must get going. Come, Solomon.'

There was a flurry of activity when Ato Alemu opened the door of his office to let us out. Everyone had been crowding round the window, staring down into the street below. They scampered back to their desks when they saw their boss.

Ato Alemu didn't seem to mind.

'How long till they get here?' he asked one young man, who had been holding a little radio close to his ear.

'They've left the airport, sir. Half an hour, I'd say.'

The goodbyes seemed to go on forever, but at last we were on our way downstairs.

Down in the street below, the mass of people was packed so tight that we could hardly force our way out through the door. The crowd swirled around us, picking us up and carrying us along with them. I'd never seen so many people close together before.

I've got to say that I was scared. I thought we were going to be crushed.

Even Grandfather looked a bit shaken. I think he was regretting that he hadn't stayed upstairs in the office, as Ato Alemu had suggested, but he'd never have admitted it and gone back inside. Anyway, we'd have had to walk up all those stairs again.

We started trying to edge along behind the crowd, sticking close to the buildings where there was a bit more space. After the first few moments, it wasn't as hard as I'd feared. People seemed to be in a good mood, talking to each other, and squeezing up to let us get past.

'Are they nearly here?' someone called out to a man listening to a little radio.

'Yes! Ten minutes maximum! They're almost at Piazza!'

When I think about what happened next, I still feel myself go cold with fright. And shame. How could I have been so stupid? How could I have forgotten the precious pouch full of money on its string round my neck? How could I have let it hang outside my shirt so carelessly?

It all happened so quickly. We were trying to get round a knot of people standing around the doorway of a shop when a ragged boy stepped between me and Grandfather. I tried to dodge round him, but the boy moved too. He was bigger then me. He had an intent, scowling look on his face.

'Please, I can't see my grand—' I began to say. The boy jerked his head up and nodded to someone behind me. At that moment, I felt a tug at my neck. I tried to turn my head, but the boy in front of me grabbed my arm, squeezing it so hard that it hurt. I was trying to wrestle him off when suddenly he turned and plunged into the crowd with another, smaller boy darting after him. A second later, they had disappeared.

I put up my hand to rub the sore place on my arm, and that's when I made a terrible discovery. The string round my neck had been cut. It was hanging loosely over my shirt. The boys must have been working together. The one behind me had cut the string. He'd stolen the pouch. My money was gone.

Chapter Nine

I was so shocked that I couldn't move a muscle. I just stood there, frozen with panic. I couldn't even open my mouth to shout. And, to make things a hundred times worse, I'd lost sight of Grandfather. He'd been swallowed up by the crowd.

I can't have been stuck like that, paralysed, for more than a moment or two, because almost at once I felt a great rush of rage. Pure rage! And I began to fight my way through the mass of people, hitting out and yelling.

The worst thing was not being tall enough to see over people's heads. I could tell, though, that there was a bit of fuss going on, further on, because people were calling out angrily, 'Hey! Mind out! Don't push! Stop that!'

I wormed my way through to where the shouts were coming from, hoping like anything that they'd stopped the thief. And then I got another shock, because someone to one side of me was calling out my name.

'Solomon! Over here! Solomon!'

I jumped up, trying to get a glimpse over the shoulder of the woman beside me, and there, just beyond her, was Kebede. He was grinning like crazy, and holding my pouch up in his hand.

I felt as if I'd been punched, as if the breath had been knocked out of me. I'd trusted Kebede. I'd *liked* him! But he was just a thief, after all, a thief who'd stolen my money. And now he was teasing me with it, laughing at me because I was a hick from the country.

With one last desperate push I got past the woman and reached him. I grabbed my pouch out of his hand and shoved my face right into his.

'You dirty thief!' I shouted at him. 'You—'

'Hey! Hey!' He put his hands up and if there'd been more room he'd have backed away from me. '*I* didn't steal your thing. I was waiting for you to come out of that office building. I thought it would be fun if we watched the procession together. I saw the kid who was tracking you, and the accomplice guy who gave you a push. I knew what they were up to, but before I could warn you one of them got out a knife and cut your purse string. The big guy went off quickly, but the smaller one, who had your pouch, got stuck in the crowd, so I gave him a good old punch in the guts and he doubled over and I grabbed your purse back. Here, give it back to me and I'll tie a knot in the string and you can put it on again. But keep it inside your shirt this time.'

I was so relieved I just handed the pouch back to him, and, like he said he would, he tied a knot in the string and slipped it back over my head. I was blushing with embarrassment. How could I have called Kebede a thief? He'd never want to be my friend now.

'I'm really sorry I said all that,' I blurted out at last. 'I thought—'

'I know what you thought, but don't bother about it now. Come on, we've got to hurry. They'll be here in a minute, and I know a really good place where we can watch the procession.'

Then I remembered Grandfather and my stomach dropped again.

'I can't! I've got to find my grandfather! He'll be going crazy!'

'It's too late for that,' Kebede said cheerfully. 'He'll be way ahead by now, and how are you going to find anyone in this crowd? You'll catch up with him again when the procession's gone by.

Come *on*! They're nearly here!'

He grabbed my arm and pulled me after him, and then I found myself right at the back of the crowd again, squashed up against a tall building.

'We won't be able to see anything from here,' I started to say, but then I saw the pipe running down the outside of the building and I got the point at once. Kebede was shinning up it already. He reached a windowsill and managed somehow to twist himself round so that he could sit on it with his legs dangling down.

'Hurry up, Solomon!' he yelled down at me. 'They're coming!'

I'm not that brilliant at climbing, to be honest. There aren't too many trees round where we live, and the ones there are get cut for firewood or fence posts as soon as they're a bit tall. But I was up that pipe as if I'd been climbing all my life. Kebede gave me his hand to help me up the last bit, and he edged further along the windowsill so that I could sit beside him.

I forgot about Grandfather. I forgot about everything, because my heart was pounding with excitement and a sort of bursting pride at being

Ethiopian, and a longing for I didn't know quite what. This was the moment the whole country had been waiting for. The Olympic Games had been a triumph for our runners again, and now the champions were returning. And I, Solomon, was there to greet them. It was the best moment in my whole life.

We could see right over the heads of the crowd. The road was empty of traffic, and all the people were crammed on to the pavements at the sides, with policemen holding them back to keep the roadway clear.

Then I heard a roaring noise, a sort of bellowing like a herd of animals, only it was people, thousands of people, cheering. It was all drowned out a moment later because there was another, much louder noise, a terrible, ear-splitting racket that scared me so much that I grabbed hold of Kebede's arm before I knew what I was doing.

'It's OK!' he yelled, right in my ear to make himself heard. 'It's only a helicopter. See?'

I looked up, and there it was, hovering overhead like a giant bird. As I watched, someone leaned out of the helicopter's open side and threw handfuls of papers down from above. They fluttered over the crowd like big white feathers, and the people below jumped up to catch them. I'd never seen anything so strange in my life. I was so fascinated I forgot about everything going on down in the street. But then the helicopter seemed to roll over on to its side and a moment later it had turned and flown off. I couldn't see it any more.

Down in the street, a whole forest of Ethiopian flags had appeared. Our national colours were everywhere, red and green and gold, draped over people's shoulders and waving in the air. I was shivering with joy.

'Isn't this great!' shouted Kebede, nudging me so hard I nearly fell off the windowsill.

Then, from far down the road, we saw them coming, bands of men. They were running. They carried poles over their shoulders with flags fluttering from them. They were shouting even louder than the cheering crowds. They came closer and closer until I could hear them.

'Ah oh!' they were chanting. 'Ah oh! Ah oh! Ah oh!'

Sweat glistened on their cheeks.

The crowd was on fire, yelling and clapping, and the women were crying out 'Alalalala!' at the tops of their voices.

And then there was the blare of motor horns and police sirens, and the rumble of engines, and several jeeps full of policemen with outriders on motorbikes came past, the sunlight glinting on their white helmets.

Suddenly they were there! They were being carried along the waves of sound. I could see them! Our heroes and heroines! Our Ethiopian champions!

There were three black cars. The athletes were standing on the back seats, their heads and chests sticking out through the sunroofs. They wore our flags, the gold and green and red of Ethiopia, draped over their brilliant green and yellow Team Ethiopia tracksuits. Garlands of golden flowers hung round their necks.

Everyone was jumping up and down, waving their arms and cheering at the tops of their voices. And then a strange thing happened. The sound seemed to fade away. My eyes had fixed on the blue ribbon round the neck of the woman in the first car. The gold medal on the end of it glittered in the sun.

I heard Kebede's voice as if from far away.

'It's her! It's Derartu Tulu! The fastest woman in the world!'

Everything seemed to slow down. Derartu Tulu turned her head, and now she was looking at me. Her eyes were on me. The moment seemed to last forever. And then she turned away.

But she *had* looked at me. She *had* smiled at me!

My skin was prickling all over and my hair was standing on end.

A moment later, they had gone, and the crowd was spilling out into the street, walking off, in every direction.

'Wasn't that great, Solomon? Didn't I get us a good place?' Kebede said.

I hardly heard him, because someone was tugging at my foot. I looked down into the angry face of a policeman.

'What are you kids doing up there? Get down here at once!'

'Sorry, sir,' said Kebede meekly. 'We're not doing any harm. We only wanted to watch.'

He turned round in one easy move, put his hands down on the sill, launched his body off, dangled in the air for a moment and dropped to the ground.

I still couldn't move. A vision had exploded in my head.

'I had to see them,' I explained seriously to the policeman. 'I had to know what it's like, because one day that's going to be me. One day, I'm going to win gold at the Olympic Games.'

Chapter Ten

Kebede had told me that you should never talk back to a policeman in Addis Ababa. They get mad at you for nothing. But it was such a special day that this policeman didn't get too angry. He even nearly smiled, and when I'd scrambled down off the windowsill he just smacked us both over the head, but lightly, and told us to hop it.

Now that the glory of seeing the athletes had gone, I was really, really worried about Grandfather. I didn't know where to start looking for him.

Kebede didn't understand at all. He was busy giving a thumbs-up sign to a friend, a boy inside a passing minibus, whose face was pressed up against the window.

'What are you so worried about?' he said, turning his attention back to me. Your grandfather'll be all right. He knows his way around. Look, you've never been to Addis before, have you? Now's your chance. I can show you the sights. You can tell your granddad you got lost and couldn't find your way back.'

I stared at him. Not even Marcos was as daring as Kebede. I'd never met anyone so bold and free before. For one mad moment I was tempted to go off with him, but I knew I couldn't.

'He – Grandfather – he's not well,' I said, afraid that I sounded lame. 'I'm supposed to be looking after him.'

Kebede shrugged, and I was afraid that he was going to run off and leave me. But then he just grinned and said, 'I'll take you back to our place, then. I bet you'll find your granddad there.'

We got back to Piazza in no time. Kebede was so fast, darting across roads between the cars and trucks, and dodging round people on the pavements, that I could hardly keep up with him. Once, I thought I was going to get squashed flat under a van that appeared from nowhere just when I'd stepped out into the road.

Then suddenly we were almost back at Kebede's uncle's shop, and my heart skipped a beat when I saw that there was a cluster of people round the door. I knew, I don't know how, that something bad had happened.

And I was right, because when we got there Kebede's uncle came out through the door, and when he saw me he grabbed hold of me and pushed me inside. He looked upset.

'Where have you been, boy? He's been needing you.'

Then he saw Kebede and frowned angrily.

'You! Running off again! You useless . . .'

But I wasn't listening to him any more because by now my eyes had got used to the darkness inside the shop (the sunshine outside had been dazzling) and I could see Grandfather. He was lying across three chairs that had been pushed together and he was quite still. For an awful moment I thought that

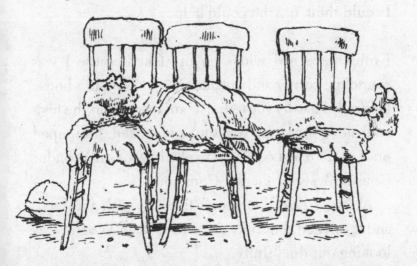

he was dead. A couple of women were beside him. One was fanning his face. The other was rubbing his hands and she turned to look at me. She must have seen what I was thinking, because she said, 'He's been unconscious, but he's coming round now. God is good!'

The other one said, 'Where's he staying? He's your grandfather, isn't he? You'll have to get him home.'

I didn't wait a moment longer but turned and dashed out of the shop. Cousin Wondu might be a cheat, trying to steal Grandfather's medal, and I knew I couldn't trust him, but he was a cousin after all, Grandfather's own nephew, and the only person I could think of who could help.

I must have had wings on my feet because I was round the corner and outside Cousin Wondu's house before I'd hardly started. The metal door in the high wall along the street was shut and locked. I thumped on it as hard as I could and yelled, 'Cousin Wondu! Cousin Meseret! Please! Come out!'

At last I heard someone fiddling with the lock, and it opened, but only a crack. Cousin Wondu was looking out doubtfully.

'What is it, Solomon? What are you making all that racket for?'

'Please, oh please . . .' I could feel a sob rising up inside my chest. 'Grandfather's been taken ill. He's really bad. He's just round the corner, in a shop. I don't know what to do!'

Cousin Wondu looked almost relieved. He'd probably expected that Grandfather would come storming back, in a furious temper, having found out about his cheating. He opened the door wide.

'I told him, didn't I, to rest today? I told him not to go traipsing about town. He didn't go far, then, only to Piazza?'

I could tell what he was up to. He wanted to find out if we'd been to Ato Alemu's office. I wasn't going to let on. I didn't want to distract him from helping Grandfather.

'Please, Cousin Wondu. Just come!'

'Wait here,' he said, and shut the door in my face.

I stood outside in the street, hopping from one leg to another and feeling so impatient that I nearly started banging on the door again. But it was only a few minutes before he came out.

'Just fetching this,' he said, holding out his mobile phone to show me. 'We might need to call a doctor.'

When we got back to the shop, I could have cried with relief. Grandfather was sitting up. He still looked awful, his head resting against the wall behind him, his mouth open and his eyes shut, but at least he was alive.

'Uncle!' Cousin Wondu put his hand on Grandfather's shoulder. 'It's me, Wondu. Can you hear me? Are you all right, Uncle?'

Of course he's not all right! I wanted to shout at him. *Can't you see that he's really ill?*

'I think he's had a heart attack,' Kebede's uncle said. 'He looks really bad. You ought to take him to the hospital. He can't stay here. He needs to be in bed.'

I could tell that he was getting a bit impatient with us. I suppose it was bad for his business, having sick people in the shop. He was a kind man, though. He still looked as if he was concerned.

Cousin Wondu didn't answer. He just started punching numbers into his phone, then he went outside the shop with it pressed against his ear.

Grandfather's head flopped over to one side. I thought he was going to topple off his chair, so I sat down beside him to prop him up.

'Grandfather!' I said softly. 'It's me. Solomon.'

I wanted to say, *Don't worry, you'll be all right*, but I didn't, because I knew he would have said, *Don't be silly, boy. Only God knows what will happen, and you certainly don't.*

So I just sat there, and waited.

Kebede's uncle had gone back behind his counter and was weighing out sugar for the woman who had been patting Grandfather's hand. The other one had gone, and the little crowd that had been hanging around waiting for something dramatic to happen had gone away too. The new customers coming into the shop hardly glanced at us, sitting in our dark corner.

I felt Grandfather's arm move, and looked up at him. His eyes were open. He'd turned towards me and was trying to say something. I couldn't make out the words. He coughed weakly, and his eyes screwed up as if he had a pain. Then he tried to talk again.

'Did . . . you tell . . . Wondu?'

'About Ato Alemu, and the medal? No, Grandfather.'

He gave a tiny nod, and I could see he was pleased. Then he looked down towards his chest.

'Take it.'

It took a moment for me to understand.

'Take what? The medal?'

He made a little grunting noise, and I could tell he was impatient with me for not understanding at once.

It felt funny, really bold and cheeky, feeling under Grandfather's shawl and sticking my fingers into his pocket, but actually it was quite easy to hook out the little box. I slid it into the pocket of my shorts.

Grandfather let his head roll back and I could tell he was relieved. He hadn't finished talking, though.

'Go home. Now. Fetch your father.'

I stared at him.

'Grandfather! I can't! I don't know the way!'

'Bus,' he croaked. 'To Kidame. Go now. Get there tonight.'

I felt sick with fright. Where would I find a bus? How much would it cost? Would they even let me on by myself?'

Cousin Wondu came back into the shop. His voice sounded stronger than it had before, as if he'd made a decision.

'I'm taking you to hospital, Uncle,' he said. 'There's a taxi waiting outside. We'll get you into a bed there, and the doctors'll see you. You'll be better in no time. Here, Solomon, help me get him up.'

It was hard heaving Grandfather to his feet. We had to almost carry him outside. He collapsed on to the back seat of the taxi, and looked worse than ever, as if he was struggling to take every breath.

Cousin Wondu was bending down to give directions to the taxi driver when Cousin Meseret came running up.

'What's going on?' she said sharply to Cousin Wondu. 'What's all the fuss about?'

I stepped back. She hadn't seen me.

'It's Uncle Demissie,' said Cousin Wondu. 'He's been taken bad. You got my message, then.'

'Yes, and I've got to get back to work. They don't like people running off in the middle of the day, I can tell you.' She bent down and peered into the taxi at Grandfather. 'He looks bad. Did he get to see . . . Does he know?'

'I don't think so,' Cousin Wondu said, 'and I hope he never finds out. I've had enough of your silly tricks, Meseret. I should never have let you put me up to it.'

'Me?' she glared at him. 'You're blaming *me*? It was your idea! You said—'

'I did not. You were the one—'

'Oh please,' I said, darting between them, 'just get him to the hospital!'

'Hospital!' exploded Cousin Meseret. 'Who's going to pay for a hospital?'

'I am,' said Cousin Wondu. 'He's my uncle, and I'm going to do the right thing for once. Here, Solomon, hop in on the other side.'

'I — I can't, Uncle,' I said, stepping back. 'He told me to go home. He wants me to go to Kidame on the bus, now, this afternoon, and fetch my father.'

Cousin Wondu looked at his watch.

'That's not a bad idea. You'll have to be quick. There's only one bus to Kidame in the afternoon. It might have gone already.'

'But I don't know where to go! Where do I get on it?' I said, feeling panicky again.

Someone tugged at my sleeve. I turned, and saw Kebede.

'I can take you to the bus station,' he said. 'I'll ask my uncle.' And he darted back into the shop.

Cousin Wondu looked relieved. He was about to say something when Grandfather began to cough. The cough turned into a groan.

'Don't worry, Grandfather. I'll be all right,' I said.

'Kebede will help me. Please, Cousin Wondu, just take him to the hospital!'

Grandfather groaned again. Cousin Wondu hesitated for a moment longer, then got into the taxi and it sped off down the street.

Kebede came out of the shop, with his uncle close behind him.

'I suppose you'll have to show the boy the way,' the old man was grumbling, 'but . . .'

Kebede's eyes were dancing.

'I know. Straight to the bus station and straight back again,' he said with a grin.

He peeped inside again to check that his uncle was busy with a customer, then lifted a few bananas off the fruit stand outside the shop.

'I'm starving,' he said. 'I bet you are too. Come on, Solomon. If you want to catch that bus, we'll have to run.'

Chapter Eleven

It was quite a long way to the bus station, but luckily it was all downhill. Kebede was as quick as a flash, darting round the people on the crowded pavements and diving across the roads between the cars and trucks. I knew I could have beaten him easily on a straight clear road, but all this city-street business, this dodging and weaving, was really hard for me.

You could tell when we were near the bus station because of the roar of the engines. My mouth dropped open when I saw the scarlet and gold buses all lined up. There were dozens and dozens of them! Some buses had just arrived, and their passengers were stepping out of them, weighted down with sacks and bags. Others were standing still with their doors closed and people crowding round, waiting to get on.

Kebede dashed over to a building on the far side, with me trying to keep up with him. There was a mass of people inside. He started worming his way through them. I stuck to him as closely as I could, but I wasn't as quick as he was, and I kept treading on people's toes and getting their elbows in my face.

I'd never have been able to get a bus ticket if Kebede hadn't been there. He made it to the front of the crowd and pushed his way right up to the counter, then held his ground while other people tried to shove him aside.

'Kidame!' he was yelling. 'One ticket!'

The man behind the counter said something and Kebede turned round and hissed, 'Get out the money!'

I fumbled in my pouch and pulled out two precious crumpled green notes.

'Not enough! Quick!'

He shoved the bananas he was still holding into my hands, grabbed the pouch, so that the string holding it round my neck pulled our heads close together, fished out more money and turned back to the counter.

A second later, the ticket was in my hand and Kebede was stuffing the notes he hadn't needed back into the pouch. I gave him back the bananas, and tucked the little leather bag carefully back inside my shirt. I was going to make sure it was safe this time.

'You'll be off in ten minutes,' Kebede said, as we made it back out into the open air. I stared round at the ranks of scarlet buses.

'Yes, but which one is it?' I said anxiously. 'What if I get in the wrong one?'

'You won't. Follow me!'

And he was off again.

My bus was at the other side of the bus station. Its

doors still hadn't opened, and I joined the mass of
people waiting to get on.

'You've been great,' I said, feeling suddenly
embarrassed. 'I could never have . . .'

'It's been fun.' He stopped. I could see that he felt
a bit awkward too.

'That money in your pouch,' he said, 'is that all
you've got? No more?'

He looked as if he was sorry for me.

'We're not poor,' I said, feeling stung. 'We've
got three good cows and Lucky – she's our donkey
and she's had a couple of foals already – and our own
fields, and my father always pays my school fees.'

'Wow! You go to school?'

'What? Don't you?'

'Course not. Who's going to pay for me?'

'Doesn't your uncle?'

'Him? No. He's not my real uncle anyway. Just a
sort of cousin.'

'Where are your mum and dad?'

He shrugged.

'They passed away. Last year.'

'Oh.' I didn't know what to say.

'You're lucky to go to school,' he said.

Up to that point, I'd been a bit jealous of Kebede,

with his shoes and his confidence and his smart city knowledge. Now I could see that he was envious of me.

It was just as well, I suppose, that the driver and conductor turned up then, ready to open the door of the bus and let everyone on, because neither of us knew what to say next.

Kebede held out two of the bananas he'd been carrying. I suddenly realized how hungry I was.

'You know what?' I said, taking them gratefully. 'I'm really sorry I've got to go home. I've had such an amazing time today.'

'Me too. Those athletes – fantastic, weren't they?'

The doors of the bus had opened.

'I've got to go,' I said as the crowd pushed me towards the steps.

'Don't worry about your grandfather,' Kebede called out, standing on tiptoe to see me over the heads of the two women behind me. 'They'll look after him in the hospital. He'll be all right, I bet.'

I felt a stab of guilt. I'd been so busy with Kebede I'd actually forgotten about Grandfather.

'Kebede!' I'd got on to the bottom step of the bus, and turned to call back to him. 'Can you do something for me? Can you go back to the Happiness

Pastry and find a man called Ato Alemu? Fourth floor in the building behind. Ethiopian Sports Company. Tell him about Grandfather being in hospital.'

'Are you getting on this bus or not?' the woman behind me said crossly, and shoved me up the next step so hard I nearly tripped. I didn't know if Kebede had heard me. When at last I'd got to the back of the bus and found myself a seat, I managed to look out of the window. He had gone. There was a boy in the distance, dodging between the buses, as fast as a darting fish, but I couldn't be sure that it was Kebede.

Chapter Twelve

The bus roared and lurched its way through the crowded streets like a mad old noisy bull. It had to stop all the time because there were other things blocking the road – donkeys and people and cars and trucks and bicycles.

I hadn't had time to look around at the other passengers when I was getting on, but now I could see a few familiar faces. I knew, now that I'd been in Addis Ababa, that Kidame was a really small place. It was obvious that I was going to recognize people from there who were on their way back home.

A woman was sitting in the seat across the aisle from me with a little boy and a little girl. The children were much younger than me. I smiled at them, and they hid their faces shyly, but when I started to eat one of my bananas they stared and stared. I finished the first one and got ready to peel the second, but their pleading looks made me feel bad. I had a bit of a struggle with myself, because I was so hungry, but in the end I couldn't resist them, so I said, 'Here you are, kids,' and handed it over the aisle to them.

They didn't say anything, but their smiles made me feel good about myself. The girl peeled the skin back and gave half to the little boy.

They had nearly finished munching their way through it when their mother, who had been looking out of the window, turned and saw what they were doing.

'Where did you get that banana?' she said sharply.

The girl pointed at me.

'Oh!' She smiled and nodded at me. 'That was nice of you.'

Then she reached down to the bag on the floor between her feet and pulled out a bundle tied in a cloth. She laid it on her knee, untied the cloth and opened the lid of one of the plastic boxes inside. A smell of home-cooked food wafted out from it, and my mouth filled up with saliva.

She held the box out to me.

'Go on. Have some.'

I took a little piece. It was delicious, a satisfying mixture of injera and spicy lentils. She shook the box under my nose again.

'No, really. You've hardly had any. Help yourself.

Finish it if you like. A boy like you – you've got to be hungry. Boys always are. Anyway, I've got plenty more.'

I didn't wait to be asked again. Anyway, once I'd started eating I don't think I could have stopped. A minute later, I'd bolted the lot. She laughed when I handed the empty box back to her, and gave me a drink of water. All in all, I thought it was a good exchange for one old spotty banana.

'Don't I know you?' she said, when she'd wrapped the empty box up and put it back in her bag. 'Don't you go to school in Kidame?'

'Yes, I do.' I suddenly felt wary. She was looking at me curiously, and I knew she'd want to get everything out of me – who my parents were, why I was alone on the bus from Addis Ababa, what I'd been doing there, who I'd been visiting, and all the rest of it.

Why didn't I want to tell her? I don't know. I suppose that Grandfather had been keeping his secrets to himself for so long that the habit had rubbed off on me. I steeled myself, ready to fend off more questions. But then the bus made an unexpected lurch. There was a knocking noise from the engine, then the roaring sound it had been making stopped. We drifted to a halt. There was a moment of total silence, then everyone started talking at once.

'Oh no! What? A breakdown? How long's this going to take?'

The conductor, who had been sitting in the front just behind the driver, got up to talk to him, then the two of them got out, and stood by the door while the driver talked into his mobile phone.

The conductor got back on, and everyone stopped talking to listen to him.

'I'm sure it's just a little temporary problem,' he said soothingly. 'My colleague here, the driver, has sent for a mechanic. He'll be with us in no time. It'll be fixed up soon, don't worry, and then we'll be on our way.'

Everyone groaned.

'It's a disgrace!' another person said. 'These old buses should be taken off the road. We've all paid for our tickets.'

I stood up and joined the people who were getting off. I was glad in a way to be outside again. It had been stuffy and cramped in the bus.

I tried listening to what people were saying all around me, to work out what was happening.

'Getting a mechanic here will take hours, and what if he can't fix the engine even when he gets here? They'll have to send a replacement bus,' a woman was saying.

'If you ask me, they won't lay one on till tomorrow morning,' said another. 'They'll tell us all to go back into town and try again tomorrow.'

Tomorrow! I thought, my heart jumping. *I can't wait till tomorrow. Grandfather might not even be alive by then.*

I looked around to try to work out where we were. The bus had come quite a distance, and we were already past the outskirts of the city. The road ran straight ahead, cutting between fields, climbing and falling over rises and dips, pointing straight towards Kidame and home. It seemed to invite me. I squinted up towards the sun. There were still four hours of daylight left.

Run it, a voice said inside my head. *You can do it. Twenty miles. Less than a marathon. Just do it.*

I took a few tentative steps away from the bus. I'd be on my own. There might be thieves. Wild dogs. All kinds of dangers I couldn't imagine.

'Where are you going?' the woman who had given me food was calling out to me. That decided me. I'd

get away from her nosy questions. I'd be out in the fresh air. I'd be on my own, doing what I did best. I'd be running.

'I'm going home!' I shouted back to her. 'Thanks for the food!'

And I took off as if I'd become the Arrow himself. I heard shouts behind me. People were calling to me to come back, not to be a little fool, to wait, like everyone else. I didn't listen. I was off.

Chapter Thirteen

I know things now about running that I didn't know back then. That day, I learned the most important thing of all, and here's what it is. Running isn't all about your legs and arms. They do the work, of course (your legs especially), but what really matters is what's going on inside your head.

You have to get your mind into a place where it's not worrying about tiredness. It's not thinking about the soreness in your feet, or the ache in your legs, or the pain in your lungs.

I didn't know then how to pace myself and I started off much too fast. I sprinted down the road, away from the bus and all the gawping passengers, as if a lion was chasing me. I had to slow down in the end, of course, because I had a stitch in my side, and I was so puffed that I could hardly breathe. It was then that I began to think. Only it wasn't just me inside my head. Grandfather was there too.

'Calm down,' I could hear him saying. 'You

haven't been stung by a bee, and there isn't actually a lion on your tail. Keep to the same pace. Nice and steady.'

Nice and steady. Nice and steady. Nice and steady.

The words repeated themselves over and over again, making a rhythm for my legs to keep to. Then, when I'd settled into my pace, a number game took over.

First I counted my strides to the top of the next rise.

One, two, three, four . . .

And when I'd reached the top, I'd count myself down the slope to the bridge over the stream in the dip below.

. . . fifty-nine, sixty, sixty-one . . .

You can't keep counting forever, though. I got really bored and lost my focus after a while. That's when the worrying took over.

What if Grandfather doesn't make it? I thought. *I've left him on his own in Addis Ababa. What if the hospital doesn't take him in? I should have gone back with all those other people when the bus broke down. I was crazy to think I could run all this way. How far have I come so far, anyway?*

My legs started to feel heavy and my pace faltered.

And then a truck came roaring up behind me, forcing me off the tarmac on to the edge of the road, where I was afraid my feet would get cut up by the sharp stones.

My chest started to heave with a sort of horrible panic. Then, just when I needed him, Grandfather came back into my head. He hadn't panicked. He'd jumped out of a truck on to the back of a horse and then he'd run for his life.

Nice and steady, Solomon, I heard him say. *Nice and steady*.

I found my rhythm again. I was running properly once more. I forced myself back to counting, not my paces, this time, but anything else I could see — the telegraph poles running alongside the road, then the birds sitting on the wires, and the farmhouses on the hillside, and the trees edging the bit of land round a church.

There wasn't much traffic luckily. Occasionally, a truck or a car came past. I easily overtook the farmers riding their donkeys, or children walking home from school. A few people called out greetings and questions to me, but mostly they left me alone. I was glad. I didn't want to waste my breath answering them.

I'd been going for what felt like hours and hours, on and on, up one hill and down the next, when I heard a familiar roaring noise behind me. I looked over my shoulder, and saw the bus! It was coming up fast. I waved at it frantically.

'Stop!' I yelled. 'It's me! I paid my fare!'

The driver didn't recognize me. He blasted his horn to get me out of the way, and raced past. I could see the passengers turning round to look at me out of the windows, and I hoped desperately that they'd make the driver stop. He didn't.

That was the worst moment of the whole day. I felt so stupid and exhausted and hopeless that I wanted to sit down beside the road, put my head on my knees and cry.

'You idiot!' I said out loud to

myself. 'You stupid, crazy fool! Why didn't you stay with the bus?'

It took much more energy and courage to get going after that. My legs felt like blocks of wood and my feet were sore and I was desperate for a drink. I had to force myself to start running again.

One, two, three . . . I began, trying to count my paces, but the magic of my number games had gone.

Fool! Fool! Stupid fool! was the only rhythm I could run to, and that didn't help much.

Just when I thought I wouldn't be able to go any further, I came over the top of a rise, and there, down in the valley below me, was the bus! It had pulled over to the side of the road and the passengers had all climbed out. The cover of the engine at the back was up, and a man was poking about inside it.

Yes! It's broken down again! I thought triumphantly. *I wasn't such a fool to leave it, after all.*

The passengers called out to me as I came alongside.

'Hey, you're the boy who decided to run it!'

'Well done!'

'We tried to tell the driver when we passed you, but he wouldn't stop.'

Someone held a bottle of water out to me.

'Have a drink. You deserve it.'

I took the bottle and gulped down the water. It tasted wonderful! It sent shivers of energy all through me.

The conductor came up to me. He was smiling.

'You can get back on if you like,' he said. 'I know you've paid to get to Kidame.'

'How long before you get going again?' I panted. I was still out of breath.

He shrugged.

'Who knows? The mechanic's doing his best.'

'How far is it to Kidame from here?'

'Only three or four miles. You've run nearly all the way.'

'I'll go on, then,' I said. 'And I bet I get there before you do.'

The passengers cheered as I took off again.

'Go for it!' they called out after me. '*Gobez!* Be strong! Run fast!'

And I was strong! I did run fast! Perhaps it was the water, or their encouragement, or knowing how far I'd already come – I don't know, but I felt different now. My pace returned. My head settled down. I concentrated on my rhythm and my legs just kept pumping up and down, eating up the miles. I was running like a champion – I knew I was.

I saw Kidame in the distance, not half a mile away, and then behind me I heard that old familiar roar.

I won't let them overtake me! I told myself. *I'll beat the bus. I will! I will!*

I wouldn't have done it if it hadn't been for the farmer who was pushing a cart loaded with sacks along the road in front of me. A truck swerved to avoid him, and somehow the farmer lost control and the cart tipped over and the sacks were scattered all over the road.

I glanced round quickly, just giving myself time to see the frantic efforts of the farmer trying to gather up his sacks, and the truck, which was stuck in the ditch with its back half blocking the road, and the red flash of the bus, bearing down on the mess, hooting away on its horn.

It'll take them ages to get past, I thought, and I found a huge rush of energy from somewhere deep inside, and I began to sprint.

I made it! I came surging down the main street of Kidame with the bus right behind me, and then I tripped over a stick someone had left lying beside the road and fell full length, my heart pounding, and my face in the dust.

Chapter Fourteen

Life is really quiet in Kidame. It doesn't take much to create a sensation, and that's what I did, all right. People always hang around when the bus is due, in case there's any news, or someone interesting gets off, so there was a bit of a crowd on the main street already.

There I was, lying down, wondering if I'd broken half my bones and if I'd ever find the strength to get up again, when I realized that a couple of boys from my school were standing over me.

'What are you doing down there, Solomon? Marcos said you'd gone to Addis. What's the matter? Can't you get up?'

I suppose I must have muttered something, and then I started struggling to stand up. They helped me to my feet. I felt dazed, half winded by my fall, weak all over with tiredness, and wanting only to lie right down again on the ground and stay here. But I knew I had to go on. I had to get home, as quickly as possible, and there were five more miles to run.

Another boy came racing up.

'I've just heard! He ran all the way from Addis. He beat the bus! Everyone's talking about it.'

People were coming at me from all sides, crowding round and asking questions. I had to get away. It would be dark soon, and I had to get home. I'd got my breath back by now.

'I didn't really beat the bus,' I said. 'Only at the end. It broke down. Ask them.'

I jerked my chin towards the clump of passengers who were still collecting their bags and bundles from the bus, and while everyone was looking away I summoned the strength from somewhere to dash down the street to the far end of town, and turn down the lane that that led home.

'Solomon! Wait! What's going on?'

I recognized Marcos's voice.

'Can't tell you now,' I called back to him over my shoulder. 'Got to get home!'

He'd have chased after me if he could, but even though I felt nearly at the end of my strength after running so far he didn't have a hope of catching up with me. He knew it. He was still shouting questions after me when I was touching the old post at the bottom of the hill, as I always did, ready to run up the slope on the far side.

Everything I'd done and seen in Addis Ababa faded away. Meeting Kebede, the stolen money and how he'd got it back for me, the Happiness Pastry, the story of Bullet and Arrow, Cousin Wondu's trickery, seeing the athletes, Grandfather's collapse – all that was unreal now. I could only think of Grandfather's face. I could only hear his voice:

Run, boy. Keep your pace. Steady now. Run.

The last two miles were miserable. My feet were sore and bruised, my legs were so tired that they were trembling and my chest was heaving as I gasped for breath.

Our house, with its familiar round walls and lopsided wooden door, was the best thing I'd ever seen in my life. It was well into the evening now, and nearly dark. I smelt rather than saw the smoke from Mother's cooking fire curling out through the thatched roof.

I was almost there when the door creaked open on its leather hinge and Mother appeared with a pan of water. She threw it out in a glittering curve, and then she looked up and saw me.

'Who's there?' she called out nervously. 'Why, Solomon! Is that you? Where's your grandfather?'

It was such a relief to be at home that I don't mind admitting that I burst into tears. I staggered inside and collapsed on the floor beside the fire, trying to control my tears. I managed to gasp out that Grandfather was ill in hospital, and that he'd told me to come home and fetch Abba, and that I'd run all the way because the bus had broken down.

My parents stared at me open-mouthed, and Konjit actually forgot to fiddle with her hair.

'You left your grandfather on his own, ill, in Addis Ababa?' Abba said at last. He was smacking his right hand down into his left, the way he always does when he's upset.

'I didn't want to! He told me to!'

'You *ran*? All the way home? On your *own*?' said Mother. She made me sit up on a stool, then she brought over a pan full of water and began to wash my feet. She'd never done that before. It felt soothing and wonderful.

'I must go to Addis straight away,' said Abba. He'd been sitting on the far side of the fire, but he jumped up, almost as if he intended to start off at once. Konjit tugged at his hand.

'It's dark, Abba. It's night-time. Nobody goes out at night time. The hyenas will eat you.'

Her voice was going all high and shrill, like it does when she gets in a panic.

'First thing in the morning,' Abba said. 'Solomon, you'll have to come with me. I won't know where to find him.'

I felt as if he'd slapped me. I was so tired that I didn't think I'd ever be able to take another step. The thought of walking all the way back to Addis was dreadful.

'He can't walk that far tomorrow,' Mother said. 'Look at his feet.'

She picked up my foot and showed it to him. When she let it go, I had a look myself. My soles were swollen and there was a bad cut on my big toe. I hadn't even noticed it.

'He'll have to come, whether he likes it or not,' Abba said. 'He can ride Lucky into Kidame, and then we'll take the bus. Now give him something to eat, woman, and let him sleep. The morning bus goes at half past six and it'll take us longer than usual, walking in the dark. We'll have to be off by half past four if we're to get to Kidame in time to get a seat on the bus.'

Mother spoilt me that evening as if I'd been a baby. She massaged my aching legs, stuffed me with as much food as I could eat, and poured out glass after glass of tea with spoonfuls of sugar from her precious hoard.

'What's Abbis Adada like, Solomon?' Konjit kept asking me. 'Did you see any lions?'

'It's Addis Ababa, not Abbis Adada, silly,' I said. 'It's big. There are lots of . . .' A gigantic yawn nearly dislocated my jaw.

'Not now,' Mother said to her. 'Let him sleep.'

And so I slept. And slept.

Chapter Fifteen

I was still fast asleep when Mother shook me awake. She had already blown the embers of the fire into a blaze and made some tea. I groaned when I tried to sit up. Every muscle in my body was stiff, and even my bones seemed to ache.

Father was outside. I could hear him talking quietly to Lucky. Donkeys like being talked to. It makes them feel safe.

He put his head round the door.

'Isn't that boy up yet? We need to get going. It's nearly half past four already.'

I stood up groggily. We don't change into night clothes in the country, so there was no need to get dressed. Mother wrapped my shawl round my shoulders and put a glass of tea in my hands.

'Drink up quickly, Solomon. Your father's getting impatient.'

I nearly scalded my mouth, but it was worth it. The tea woke me up. My first thought was, *I can't go all the way back to Addis today! I'm too tired.*

My second thought was, *But I'll be riding Lucky. Abba's never let me go so far on her before. And we'll be going on the bus.*

My third thought was, *Maybe I'll see Kebede again.*

And way down at number four, I thought, *Grandfather! He might be dead by now!*

I was ashamed that Grandfather was only at thought number four, especially when I realized, even though it was pitch dark outside, how anxious Abba was. Grandfather was thoughts number one to ten for him. Nothing else counted. I'd never known him to be so impatient.

'Are you going to take all day?' he barked at me, as I hobbled over to Lucky and scrambled on to her back. 'Do you *want* us to miss the bus?'

Mother passed a piece of injera up to me.

'Eat it as you go along,' she said. 'God go with you. And take care!'

There was still more than an hour to go before the first sign of dawn. Luckily the moon hadn't set. It wasn't full, but even half a moon gives out more light than no moon at all. I thought I knew every centimetre of the path into Kidame, but I'd never gone along it in the dark before and I was afraid that Lucky would trip over stones or crash into a thorn hedge. I should have had more faith in her. She knew the way even better than Abba and I did.

She went really slowly at first, not being used to the dark, and I heard Abba tutting anxiously behind me. The first part of the way into Kidame was steep and stony. The path was so narrow that two people couldn't walk together. We had to go in single file. But once we were down on the broader, flatter bit of the path Lucky set off at a great old pace, shaking me to bits. Abba had to walk fast to keep up with her. He could walk alongside me too, now that the path was broader.

'Now tell me everything again,' he said. 'From the beginning. What happened exactly?'

So I did. I told him about Cousin Wondu's house, and how he hadn't been too pleased to see us. I told him about meeting Ato Alemu and his story of the Bullet and the Arrow, and about Grandfather jumping on to that horse out of the moving truck.

'Did all that really happen, Abba?' I asked him.

'It's the first I've heard of it, but knowing your grandfather it doesn't surprise me at all.'

'Why didn't he tell you? If it had been me, I'd have wanted to tell everyone!'

Father thought for a minute.

'I knew he was in trouble and needed to hide out in the country. Back in those days, after the revolution, everyone was scared of everyone else. I was only a little kid then. If he'd talked about what had happened, I'd probably have blabbed about it all over the place. Later, I suppose, being quiet about the past just became a habit. I don't know why he wanted to bring it all up again. Why did he want to see this Ato Alemu anyway?'

So I told him about the medal, and about how Cousin Wondu had tried to get hold of it first.

'That Wondu!' he said, sounding disgusted. 'He always was weak and silly. Trust my father to get the better of him!' He rubbed his finger along the side of his nose. 'This medal. It's valuable, then, is it? Really valuable? Did they say how much it's worth?'

The sky had turned from black to a dull grey and the stars were going out. Over on the eastern horizon, a stripe of pink was showing. It grew brighter minute by minute as the sun rose behind the distant hills. It was easier to see the path ahead now.

I didn't want to answer Abba's question. I knew

what he was thinking. He was turning the medal into money in his mind, just like Cousin Wondu had done. He was thinking of all the things he needed: a new plough, another cow, a school uniform for Konjit. I was glad I'd had the sense to take it out of the money pouch before I'd left home, and tuck it into a corner of the shelf behind Mother's coffee pot.

I wanted to get his mind going on another tack, so I rushed on to telling him about the athletes, and what it had been like seeing them. I didn't say much about Kebede. I didn't think, somehow, that Abba would approve of him. And I hated admitting that I'd lost sight of Grandfather, and hadn't found him again till after he'd collapsed, and was lying down on chairs in the shop.

'What's this hospital they've taken him too, then?' he said, when at last I stopped talking.

I was relieved. I was afraid he'd let me have it for abandoning Grandfather.

'I don't know,' I said.

'Well, how do you propose to find him, then?' snapped Abba, sounding really worried again.

'Cousin Wondu knows where the hospital is. He took him there. I can show you where his house is.

He'd tell us, wouldn't he, even if he tried to cheat us?'

I'd been through all that in my mind already. I'd planned how I'd show Abba the way from the bus station to Piazza (I was pretty sure I could remember it), and then confidently take him right to Cousin Wondu's house. I was looking forward to that bit — showing off how well I knew my way around Addis Ababa.

Abba looked anxiously up at the sky. The edge of the sun had just appeared over the far hills. Even

the tiniest sliver of its fiery rim flooded the whole
world with light. In a few minutes, it would be right
up away from the horizon, and the day would have
properly begun.

'We're late,' Abba said. 'If we don't hurry, the
bus will have filled up and we won't get on it.'

'What'll we do with Lucky?'

'Old Ahmed will look after her. He'll do anything
for a bit of money.'

Everyone knows old Ahmed in Kidame. He sits at
the side of the road all day waiting for someone to
give him something to do.

'Get off Lucky, Solomon,' Abba said. 'She's tired.
She's slowing down. Sore feet or no sore feet, we'll
have to run the last bit.'

The first few steps were agony, but I ran off the
stiffness after a bit, and I forgot about my sore feet.
I'd caught Abba's anxiety off him. We *had* to get to
Grandfather today! We *had* to get to Addis! We *had*
to be on the bus!

We got there in time, but only just. The bus
was waiting with its doors open, and people were
climbing on board. There were only three seats left,
at the very back.

'Ahmed!' Abba yelled to the old man, sitting on

a stone outside the bar. 'Look after my donkey for me, will you? I've got to go to Addis.'

'Addis!' said old Ahmed, pretending to grumble. 'Everyone's always going to Addis,' but he happily took hold of Lucky's bridle, and led her away.

My foot was already on the bottom step of the bus and Abba was right behind me, urging me on, when I heard someone shout, 'Solomon!'

I pretended I hadn't heard.

It's only some old nosy parker wanting to know how I beat the bus from Addis, I thought, but then the person called again. He sounded really urgent, and something familiar in his voice made me hesitate and turn round.

'Get on with you! Don't take all day!' said Abba, giving me a shove.

But I'd recognized that voice now. I wormed my way back down the steps and jumped off the bus.

'Ato Alemu!' I said, astonished. 'What are you doing here?'

'I've come to fetch you in my car,' Ato Alemu said briskly. 'I'm going to take you back to Addis. Your grandfather's very ill, I'm afraid. He needs you with him now.'

Chapter Sixteen

I know I ought to have been thinking about nothing but Grandfather, but I can't help admitting that I enjoyed that ride back to Addis. Ato Alemu's car was small, but that didn't bother me. It was the first time I'd ever been in one, and I thought I was the best. Royalty.

Abba sat in the front with Ato Alemu and I was in the back. Abba didn't say anything at first, and I knew he was feeling shy and strange. He hadn't taken in exactly who Ato Alemu was, and why he'd bothered to come all the way out to Kidame to pick us up. Everything was moving too fast for him. He was scared of looking ignorant and stupid.

Ato Alemu kept looking sideways at him as he drove along. I think he realized how confused Abba was feeling.

'Solomon's friend came to find me,' he said, starting to explain.

That didn't help. I hadn't told Abba much about

Kebede. I was afraid, I suppose, that he'd disapprove of him.

'Solomon's friend?' Abba sounded more mystified than ever.

I leaned forward.

'Kebede. He was the boy who took me to the bus station.'

'*Ishi*, all right,' said Abba. He was pretending to understand, I knew.

So Ato Alemu went quietly through everything again, telling the story about his own father and Grandfather being such friends, and the medal.

I could tell that Abba was beginning to feel impatient, but was trying to be polite and not show it.

'But how is he now? How's my father now?' he burst out at last. 'It looked like a heart attack, Solomon said.'

Ato Alemu hesitated.

'I went to the hospital and saw him yesterday afternoon, as soon as I heard,' he said at last. 'They're doing everything they can. We can only trust in God.'

We'd never have managed without Ato Alemu. We probably wouldn't have got in through the hospital doors. And, even if the strict-looking doormen had let us through, we'd never have found our way down those long corridors, with so many rooms leading off them.

My grandfather had always been a giant to me. I don't mean that he was very tall, or anything like that. He'd just been the head of the family. The person we respected more than anyone else. And feared, I suppose.

Grandfather had always known what to do. He would advise Abba on when it was the right moment to start bringing in the harvest. He knew how to treat Lucky when she went lame. He'd insisted on sending me to school, even when money for the fees was so tight that we'd had to cut down on food.

Nobody had ever argued with Grandfather, or answered him back.

I'd learned more about him in the last twenty-four hours than I'd known in the whole of my life. I wish more than anything that I'd had the chance to find out more.

I nearly didn't recognize him, lying so still on the bed under a sheet that was pulled up to his chin. He looked small. His face had gone the same peculiar grey colour it had been in Kebede's uncle's shop.

He was asleep. His eyes were closed and his mouth was half open.

Abba looked almost stunned by the shock of seeing him there like that.

'*Ai-ee!*' he wailed, and dropped his head into his hands.

Ato Alemu walked down the ward past ranks of beds with sick people lying in them. A crowd of relatives sat beside each one. He brought back a couple of plastic chairs and gently helped Abba into one. He didn't want to sit down himself. He pointed to the other one, and I perched gingerly on the edge of the seat.

Another shock to me was how helpless Abba seemed to be. I'd never seen him in such a state before, rocking backwards and forwards, sucking the air in through his teeth, muttering prayers and heaving tearful sighs.

I honestly thought, what with Grandfather lying so still, that his life had gone out already, but then he opened his eyes, gave a feeble little cough, turned his head, and saw us. He pulled his hand out from under the sheet, and started plucking at it. He looked agitated.

Ato Alemu knew what to do. He lifted

Grandfather's head up and tucked the pillow under it, then he picked up a cup of water from the shelf nearby and held it to Grandfather's mouth.

Grandfather's lips trembled as he tried to drink, and some of the water trickled down his chin, but a bit must have gone in because I saw his Adam's apple go up and down as he swallowed. The water seemed to do him some good.

'You came,' he said, in a faint voice.

'Yes, Father,' Abba said. 'I'm here. Solomon fetched me. He ran all the way home from Addis.'

Grandfather's eyes shifted from Abba to me.

'I did get on the bus, like you told me to;' I said, afraid that he'd be annoyed. 'But it broke down before we'd even got out into the country.'

Something sparked in Grandfather's eyes. I thought, though I couldn't be sure, that it was pride.

'Good lad,' he said. 'You're a good lad.'

I wouldn't have believed my ears if he hadn't said it twice. He'd never praised me before, not once in my whole eleven years.

'The med . . . med . . .' he murmured.

'What's that?' said Abba, leaning forward.

'The medal, I think,' I said. I leaned forward too. My head was close to Grandfather's now.

'I've got it safe,' I told him. 'I took it home.'

His mouth twisted a bit. I think he was trying to smile.

'It's yours, boy,' he whispered. 'For you. Keep.'

He seemed to be dropping off again. Ato Alemu leaned over the bed.

'Solomon's a runner, Arrow. He ran a marathon yesterday. No one can believe it. A boy of eleven.'

Grandfather's eyes flickered open.

'Runner. Good. Run. Steady pace. Eye on the finishing line. Keep on. Nearly . . .'

He didn't say any more.

A nurse came up. She held his wrist for a moment, but she didn't look at us. She just walked away.

We sat for a long time beside Grandfather's bed. Ato Alemu went away and came back with some food for us, but we didn't want to eat it. He walked down the ward again and talked to other people, leaving us alone with Grandfather. Abba sat without moving. I don't think he took his eyes off Grandfather's face for a single second.

I felt lost, to be honest. The hospital was so strange, and everyone seemed so busy, there was such a clatter of trolleys being pushed about, and nurses calling to each other, that I felt confused and frightened.

Ato Alemu came back and talked quietly to Abba from time to time. I couldn't hear what they said.

Another nurse came and held Grandfather's wrist, as the first one had done.

'Is he going to get better?' I blurted out, louder than I'd meant to.

'Pray to God,' was all she said.

We all saw the change when it came. Grandfather's eyes suddenly opened wide and he began to breathe noisily. I thought it meant that he had woken up and was going to talk to us again. I was wrong. The harsh breaths stopped.

Abba jumped to his feet and stared down at Grandfather with a dreadful look on his face.

'What's happened? Has he died?' I said stupidly.

'God has taken him,' answered Ato Alemu. 'The Arrow has gone to God.'

And he reached out his hand, and gently pulled Grandfather's lids down over his lifeless, staring eyes.

Chapter Seventeen

I felt a peculiar mixture of things in those slow-moving hours after Grandfather died. There was a sort of emptiness, and horrible regrets that I'd never known how to talk to him properly while he was alive. At the same time, I felt excited, in a strange kind of way. Everything around me was changing, and I was needed in a way I'd never been needed before.

Abba seemed as if he'd been struck down. It was frightening to see how helpless he was. Ato Alemu told me to guide him back through the hospital and out to the entrance. We were to wait for him there. He stayed behind to arrange things.

We'd just gone out down the steps and were standing outside, not knowing what to do, when Cousin Wondu appeared. He saw me first and started towards me, but then he noticed Abba, and hesitated. I didn't know what to think about Cousin Wondu by this time. He'd tried to cheat us, but he'd seemed to be sorry too. He'd brought Grandfather to the hospital, after all, and promised to pay his bill. I could see that he was feeling guilty and anxious.

'Here's Cousin Wondu,' I said to Abba.

Abba didn't hear me. He was still too shocked to take anything in.

Cousin Wondu looked as if he was screwing up his courage as he came up to us.

'I can see by your faces – has something happened?' he said.

'Grandfather passed away,' I mumbled. It didn't seem right to say it out loud.

Cousin Wondu struck the side of his head with the palm of his hand.

'I did what I could!' he said. 'I tried to make him rest at home, and then when he collapsed I brought him to the hospital. They promised to do everything for him. This is so bad, so bad!'

Abba came to life a bit. His eyes focused on Cousin Wondu. He started to say something. But I didn't listen. I'd seen something else. A boy was outside the railings that surrounded the hospital. He'd stuck his arms through them and was waving at me. It was Kebede. I ran over to talk to him.

'The doormen wouldn't let me in through the

gates,' Kebede said. 'They're really mean here. What's going on? I went back to the bus station to meet you off the bus from Kidame this morning, but you weren't on it. I heard about your marathon run. Everyone's talking about the boy who beat the bus. I went to Ato Alemu's office again, but they told me that he'd gone to Kidame to fetch you. I knew you'd be here to see your grandfather.'

I shook my head.

'He passed away. Just now.'

It wasn't any easier to say the second time.

'*Ai-ee!* Just like that! But he walked all the way to Addis Ababa only two days ago. I can't believe it!'

'I can't believe it either,' I said, but I knew even as the words came out that they weren't true. I did believe – I *knew* – that Grandfather had died. I'd seen the spirit pass out of him. I'd seen Ato Alemu close his lifeless eyes.

'What are you going to do now?' Kebede asked.

'I don't know.'

There was a shout from the gate. One of the guards had seen Kebede.

'Hey, you! Boy! What do you want? Go away!'

Kebede stepped back from the railing.

'Like I said, they're really mean here. Look, Solomon, I'll help you any way I can.'

'I know you will.'

'Don't go home without telling me.'

'I won't.'

That was the moment when we became true friends, and we're friends still and always will be. Kebede's running his cousin's shop now. I visit him every time I come home to Addis Ababa. Marcos and Kebede. My two friends for life.

I don't like remembering the next few days.

We buried Grandfather that same afternoon in the cemetery at the edge of the city. If he'd died at home, dozens of people would have followed his coffin, but no one knew him here in Addis Ababa. There was only Ato Alemu, Cousin Wondu, Abba and me.

I knew already, as we walked away down the hillside, leaving Grandfather there for all eternity, that his death had brought about great changes for me. I knew that my old life was over forever. It was almost as if he had planned it.

He couldn't have done, of course. He couldn't have known that he would fall ill. He couldn't have known that the bus would break down and that I'd run all the way home. I don't suppose he knew that Ato Alemu's sports-equipment business sponsored young runners at the special school for athletes, and that they would go on and sponsor me. He couldn't have known that I would graduate from there, a fully fledged athlete.

And how could he have known that his father's medal would be my inspiration, my lucky charm, my talisman?

Perhaps, after all, he did know all of those things. Perhaps he knew everything, and planned it that way. Underneath all his harshness, he was the wisest man I've ever met, after all.

'Your grandfather always knew you were a runner,' Abba told me recently.

We were sitting at the table in my house. He had come up from Kidame to visit me, bringing some of Ma's delicious home-cooked food. He loves to stay with me, visit the city and hear all about the races I've been running and the people I've met. Sometimes he comes to watch me train. He's even made friends with Cousin Wondu, who's been a much nicer person since Meseret went off with her boss, leaving her daughter, who's a shy teenager now, for Cousin Wondu to bring up.

'Yes, your grandfather knew you were a runner,' Abba said again. 'He used to stand at the door and watch you race off to school, screwing his eyes up to study your form till you were away down at the bottom of the hill and halfway up the other side. Sometimes he'd even give you little jobs to hold you up, so that you'd have to run fast in case you were late for school.'

'Is that why he did it?' I laughed. 'It used to drive me crazy. Why didn't he say I could be a runner? Why didn't he admit he was sort of training me?'

'That wasn't his way. He knew, anyway, that I wouldn't have approved. After all, I'd always thought that you would stay at home and help me on the farm.'

I didn't answer at once.

'Are you sorry I went away, Abba?' I said at last.

He frowned, and for a moment he looked like Grandfather.

'Don't talk such foolishness. How could I regret it? Look at you now!' He jerked his chin towards the drawer in the cupboard behind the table. He didn't have to say anything. I knew what he wanted. We go through the same ritual every time.

I stand up, open the drawer and bring out my medals, laying them side by side on the table. There aren't many yet, but I'm slowly adding to my hoard.

'And the old one,' Abba says.

I pull the little box out of the inner pocket where I always keep it, take off the lid and lift the layer of cotton wool. The disc of brown medal might look small and dowdy to a stranger. It's worth the world to me.

Abba puts out a finger and touches it reverently. I don't need to. I know exactly how it feels. I would recognize it on the darkest night if someone put it into my hand.

I'm trying to be worthy of it, Arrow, I say in my head. *I'm your grandson, after all.*

The plane has landed at last. The wheels touched down on the runway a few minutes ago. We've come to a halt near the terminal, and the ground staff are bringing up the steps. The cabin crew are standing by the door, ready to open it as soon as they get the go-ahead.

We're all really excited. I'm a bit nervous too. There's a huge crowd out there. I could see their faces pressing up against the glass windows of the terminal as we taxied past.

It's my first time coming home as part of Team Ethiopia. We're all in our national strip — green and yellow — and us lucky ones have got our medals hanging on ribbons round our necks.

I'm sitting next to Derartu Tulu. She knows how I feel. She's come home to cheering crowds many times before. She's one of the greatest runners in the world. Two gold medals are clinking away on the strings round her neck. I've got one medal, and it's bronze. That's good enough for me. For now.

What Derartu doesn't know (and no one else does either) is that I've got another medal, a secret one, stitched into an inside *pocket. It's my most precious possession, and it brings me all my luck.*

The cabin doors have swung open. My heart's beating fast. Out of the window, I can see the welcoming committee and the TV crews and all the bigwigs who have been allowed out of the terminal and on to the tarmac. They're clustering round the bottom of the steps, ready to cheer us when we come out.

A posh car has driven up now. There are loads of policemen holding everyone back.

'That's the president,' says Derartu, leaning across me to look out of the window. I swallow hard, and she pats my hand. 'Come on, Solomon. You'll be fine.'

The most famous of our athletes, the nation's darlings, go down the steps first, but it takes so long for them to greet the president and move off the bottom step that I get stuck behind them, halfway down.

I look across the heads of the crowd. Security is very tight at Addis Ababa airport. No one without a permit is allowed to go airside. But a boy seems to have got through. He's wearing ragged old shorts and his feet are bare. He's hiding behind a catering truck, but I can see his face. He's staring at me, right at me, and I know (although he's too far away to be sure) that there's a hungry, longing look in his eyes.

I'd much rather talk to him than to all the officials and big shots waiting below. I raise my hand to wave to him. Shyly, he waves back, but a security guard sees him and starts to run towards him. I hold my breath. I don't want him to be caught!

The boy runs like a hare on his bare feet and disappears into the back of a loading bay. The guard hasn't a hope of catching him.

He's a runner, I think. A natural. I was just like him once. He is just like me.

Turn the page to read an extract of the classic story by

ELIZABETH LAIRD

ORANGES
IN NO MAN'S
LAND

ONE

I WAS BORN IN BEIRUT. It had been a lovely city once, or so Granny told me. The warm Mediterranean Sea rolled against its sunny beaches, while behind the city rose mountains that were capped with snow in the winter. There were peaceful squares and busy shops and hotels bustling with tourists.

My father and mother were farmers. They came from the countryside south of the city. They'd been happy in their little village. But they lost everything when Lebanon, our country, was invaded. They had to run away to Beirut, the capital. They had three children there: me first, and then my two brothers.

My father built a little house with his own hands in the poorest part of town, where everyone was crowded together in narrow lanes. All our neighbours were like us – refugees from southern Lebanon – trying to manage on nothing, but thankful at least to be safe.

But just after I was born, all that changed. A terrible civil war tore the city of Beirut apart. I pray that those years never come again! I can never forget the horror of them.

And yet, in amongst all the sad things, the fear and destruction and loss, there are wonderful memories too, of kindness and courage and goodness.

I'll have to start my story, though, with the saddest thing of all.

Ours was a house of women and children, my granny, my mother and my little brothers Latif, who was seven, and Ahmed, who was still only a baby. My father was abroad most of the time, looking for work. He'd been gone for so long we were used to him being away. I'd almost begun to forget what he looked like.

When, on that terrible day, the bombs started to fall all around our house, my mother threw some clothes into a bundle and began to pack bags and cases.

'There's no time for that!' Granny screamed at her, looking out anxiously into the street. 'The gunmen are coming! They'll be here any minute. We must take the children and run!'

Mama went on packing. She pushed a big bag into my hands and a smaller one into Latif's. Granny was already running down the street with Ahmed in her arms.

'Go on, Ayesha,' Mama said to me. 'Go with Granny. I'll be right behind you. Wait for me by the mosque on the corner.'

And so we ran, Latif and me, racing ahead of Granny, who was hobbling along behind us with Ahmed in her arms. And a shell fell on our house just as we reached the end of the street, wiping out our little shack of a house and everything in it. I never saw Mama again.